STAR DEFENDERS

ASCENSION GATE 3

JUSTIN SLOAN

ELDER TREE PRESS

WELCOME

Thank you for taking a chance on my books. I hope you love reading them as much as I loved writing them!

Justin Sloan

Last time, in Star Legacy (Ascension Gate 2):

In the second book of the Ascension Gate series, each point of view character found themselves advancing.

Trent had quite the adventure. He was tested and found deserving, might have started falling for his dragon friend, and uncovered a group of subversives based out of nearby hills.

Espinoza and the stranded Marines continued to fight for survival against sandworms and vampires, truly figuring out the key to survival when they find an unexpected friendship. It's more than that, though, as Espinoza found himself transformed—and uncovered a portal to the Goldies' world.

Shrina found her sister, but in the process awakened a dragon and learned more about her new form, and where it came from.

From there, you can imagine where their powers will take them!

ESPINOZA, KRASTIAN

Most people would have thought being stranded on an alien planet with murderous flying aliens and sandworms would be the worst possible situation. For Espinoza, though, the whole situation was mostly perfect.

For one, he was a vampire now, which meant that, in spite of the craving for blood whenever his energy was low, he could feed off the Goldies and this then gave him the ability to fly. *You're welcome, childhood Espinoza*, he thought while considering this perk amid scooping out chicken goop from an MRE. Then there was the fact that he had both Ellins *and* Kim into him. Not just one woman, but two. *You're welcome, teenage Espinoza.* He laughed, took another bite, and tried to imagine it was a Thanksgiving feast back home.

A glance over at Kim showed that she knew exactly where his mind was. "No chicken and rice MRE has ever made a man smile so goofily," she said, taking a bite of her cracker with peanut butter. "You're not still focused on—"

"Hush," Ellins interrupted, glancing around at the others in the cave. Franco was sleeping and the Goldie sat perfectly still, while Ruan, Levin, and Marick were out on patrol. "Don't need... that... being gossiped about."

For another moment, Espinoza grinned at the two of them, remembering the taste of Ellins's lips before he'd turned to press his own lips to Kim's neck, the way they had both run their hands over him, both... enjoyed him. At the same time. Back on Earth, that sort of thing simply didn't happen.

His blissful memory faded with the hint of gold at the corner of his eye. Here, on the planet they had started referring to as Krastian—after the term Earth had given this galaxy—there was that damn Goldie to deal with. Eyeing it, Espinoza lost all thoughts of his little adventures with the two ladies. That thing was creepy. No eyes, but empty sockets, kind of. Twice as large as most men, skin glowing as if molten gold moved within. This one had robes, sort of, though they seemed to consist of that same golden material that made up the rest of the being. Even sitting there, those robes flowed as if pushed by a wind that hadn't reached them yet.

More than once the group had tried to crack the Goldie, with Marick, Ruan, and Espinoza taking turns feeding from him, attempting to ask questions. So far, nothing had worked.

When the patrol returned, they had news of a storm off in the distance, but nothing aside from that. So while they checked comms, Espinoza went over to the cave entrance and stared out, wondering when the next storm would hit. Wondering how they would make it through the portals, and connect with whoever lived on the other side.

"Dreaming big dreams?" Franco asked as he joined Espinoza at the cave entrance.

"Only the biggest."

Franco chuckled at that, motioning over his shoulder toward Ellins. "I hear you there. You know I'm thinking..." He lowered his voice, mischievously. "Thinking of making a move on the Gunny."

Images of Franco with Ellins came hard and fast, the two of them licking each other's faces and tearing each other's clothes off like animals. Nothing nice about those thoughts, and an intense territorial sense of wanting to go on the attack came over Espinoza. In spite of his fists balling up, he simply smiled.

"I wouldn't."

"What? Why?" Franco frowned. "Dude, that frater-nization bull doesn't apply anymore. You realize we're stranded? Sure, we're in contact with Earth now, kind of. But who's to say they'll even make it out here if they send reinforcements? And that's a big 'if'. So... it's on us to survive, and I'm thinking she could give me a will to live, if you know what I mean."

"Dude..." Espinoza looked back at Ellins, giving her a nod. Damn, she didn't want it known about the three of them, and Franco knew that he had already hooked up with Kim. So basically, he was going to have to let the guy try with Ellins? He knew he shouldn't feel jealous at the idea, because it wasn't like she would go for him.

Even if she did, what was that to Espinoza? Wasn't it selfish to want to keep both ladies for himself? He didn't even know if they considered it anything more than a one-night deal, but whatever. With a frown, he waved off the topic.

"Can we talk about something else? Food you're going to eat when you get home—you know, once we've puked out all these MREs."

Franco laughed. "Me, I'm a true fan of the Reuben."

"Sandwich, or that pig from the Telltale Minecraft game?"

"What? They named a pig Reuben?" He frowned. "That's jacked up. But yeah, the sandwich. There was this place called The Oinkster, been around for hundreds of years, or at least, there was one a long time ago. Not sure it's the same. They do the best Reuben on Earth, guaranteed."

"I don't know, I've had some good ones."

"You're a Reuben man?"

"Aren't we all?" Espinoza shrugged. "What? Pinned me for tamales? Those too, but I'm more of a breakfast sandwich kind of guy."

"What? Like... eggs and bacon on bread?"

Espinoza felt his stomach rumbling at the thought. "There was this place that did it on a croissant—eggs, bacon, and cheese—and it was to die for. At this moment, I'd consider it."

"Of course, since you're a vampire... you would just get back up again."

A laugh burst out, but Espinoza shook his head. "Not really, though. I mean, maybe there was some truth to the idea of vampires back in the day, right? What with being able to heal and all like we are now. But no, what we are now isn't that."

"You haven't tried dying to find out."

"Haven't jabbed a stake through my heart either, but I'm not about to try."

"I've never had anything fancy like that," Franco admitted, eyes off in the distance. "That said, there was a girl I dated who loved those French pastries. Are they called pastries? The little fruit tart things, you know, with the raspberries and blueberries, the ones that aren't too sweet... Just right."

"Yeah, I think I tried one of those before."

"Man that was basically her. Not overly pretty, to the point where I felt inferior or anything weird like that. But just the right amount of pretty, just the right amount of sweet, just the right amount of kinky."

"Not something I need to hear about." Espinoza grinned. Still, not something he might mind hearing about either.

"Nothing raunchy man, I mean, not with certain ears listening." He nodded back toward Ellins. "But there was one time, she told me we were going to go get one of those tarts. I mean, I wasn't that excited exactly, but she brought me to this little bakery, and it turned out she had the whole place to herself. Her friend was going to be opening that day, but needed her to take over for a minute while she ran some errands for her grandpa or something. So she gets me back behind the counter right, takes on those tarts..." Franco leaned in then, lowering his voice. "She starts rubbing the tart in certain places, you get my drift?"

"It's hard to miss."

"Right, even puts the raspberry and the blueberries on the tip, like some sort of dress up toy. Then she goes down on me right there."

"Dude..."

"I know, right? But that's not the craziest part. I'm standing there behind the counter when this guy comes in. Orders a fruit tart right there. He can't see what she's doing, so I just take a fruit tart from the case, handed it over, and told him it's my treat. The guy walks out of there never knowing what was really happening. Best tart ever."

"I'll never look at them the same, again" Espinoza said, chuckling.

"Your turn."

"How?"

"Come on, share some dirt. Maybe about you and Kim...?"

"Not going to happen." Espinoza glanced back over his shoulder at Kim who was working at the comms again, wondering what she would think about Franco knowing anything they had done, aside from his own imagination.

"Don't be a prude, dude." Franco nudged him. "You want another story from me, to seal the deal? Okay, so same girl, right? We're headed down to the beach…"

Espinoza glanced back again, this time at Ellins, and after a moment realized that Franco wasn't talking anymore. He really didn't need to hear the story, but it was weird that Franco wasn't talking. He was about to apologize, not meaning to make the guy feel like he was being ignored, but then he saw that Franco was staring out into the distance with his mouth gaping open. Even out of the corner of Espinoza's eye, he saw why.

Turning to stare, he said, "Everyone, time to get ready."

Out in the distance, but moving in fast, was a storm different from any they'd seen before. This one had crackling gold flashes of lightning, bursts of that same light exploding out like fireworks. The base of it was dark blue, the rest of it bright orange, and the ground beneath it seemed to be undulating.

As it grew closer, the others came up close behind Espinoza, and then the whole cave started to shake and rumble.

"They're coming for him," Ellins said. They all turned back to look at the Goldie, who was sitting up straighter with his face pointed in their direction. "Prepare yourselves ladies and gentlemen, it's going to be a long night."

It was at that moment that Marick and Ruan returned, charging in... blood splattered across Marick.

"Where's Levin?" Ellins asked.

Marick shook his head, looking out to the storm. "Dead."

2

SHRINA, WASHINGON, D.C.

S tupid poster with that cat hanging onto that tree branch and looking at Shrina with pleading eyes. "Hang in there," it said. But that damn cat didn't know about the lost ships in space, the vampire attacks, or the fact that Alicia had gone off with the risen dragon.

Adding lemon juice to the cut was the fact that Shrina now stood in one of the bunkers of the Pentagon after the place had been half-destroyed. She was being held against her will, as security tried to figure out what exactly had gone down. Considering the fact that she had dragon scales, wings, and horns... they were having a hard time taking the secretary's word that she wasn't with the vampires who had led the attack.

And on top of all that, the secretary's nephew was involved. He had led the effort to wake the dragon. Cody, that jackass! He had betrayed humanity. And to think Veles had been trying to introduce them for a date at one point. She still couldn't believe his own nephew had killed him.

A cold chill ran up her spine at the thought of what it would have meant if she had ended up in bed with the traitor. Although, now that she considered it, maybe she would have learned of his plans earlier and been able to put a stop to it. Weighing that possibility against the idea of letting that slug put his slimy hands on her, though? No thanks.

"They'll see you now," a Marine said, opening the door to the back room.

She turned, ignored him, and stomped into the room. "I don't have time for this."

"You don't have a choice." The staff sergeant behind the desk sat up straight, clearly trying to look professional, but his hand shook, eyes unable to meet hers. "What was the purpose of your attack?"

"Give her a break," a voice cut in, and she blinked in confusion to see Veles. He stood there, completely alive, with two aides. "I've told you—"

"Do you want me to ask you to leave, Mr. Secretary?" The staff sergeant made eye contact with him, no problem. Apparently, it was the dragon aspects of Shrina that made him uncomfortable.

Playing with that, she thrust out her wings, smiling to show her pointed teeth. "We're on the same side. And right now, the enemy is getting away. Now, you can sit here and play twenty questions, or I spy, or whatever you want, but I mean to stop them."

"You will answer my questions and—"

She slammed her fist on the desk—metal—making a dent. "He has my sister. Those sons of bitches have her again, and this time..." She didn't know where to go with that. This time, it was different. While before they had said her sister, Alicia, had information they needed, now it was the dragon who had taken her. For what purpose?

With a sigh, the Marine eyed her up and down before finally making eye contact with, first her, and then Veles. "We're the United States Government. We have our own people to answer to, and then there's Global Command. What in the hell makes you think we can possibly release a... demon-looking lady out into the world after what just happened?"

"Demi-dragon," Shrina corrected him.

"As in, you believe you're part dragon?"

She let out a grunt of exasperation, but figured it was best to lay it out for this guy. "Listen, Staff Sergeant." She pulled back, hands behind her back to appear less threatening, even folding her wings back to reinforce that message. No tail, at least. "I am part dragon, and the man they released is a dragon of sorts. The Dragon. Used by some in your government for genetic-modification research, to create the super-soldier serum that upgraded soldiers first for New Origins and the likes, and now our own Marines and others." On those words, her eyes went to Veles, and he nodded. It suddenly made sense—of course he would have upgraded himself. As she had been reborn, apparently so had he. "I, for example," she continued, "received this serum, and when I was bitten and left for dead by the vampires, I was reborn as—er, I woke as this." She held out her hands, looking at the purplish scales on the back of them, the claws. "Likewise, the vampires are nothing more than the original batch of soldiers, and those they have infected. It was all derived from this man, the dragon."

"You're saying we created the vampires?" The Marine looked at her skeptically. "And that they're basically... some sort of dragon hybrid mutation?"

"I am. Or aliens that resemble dragons."

His eyes moved along her body, to her wings, ears, and hands. Shifting in his seat, he eyed the others in the room and seemed about to laugh. Instead, he looked down, let out a bit of a whimper, and said, "Well, son of bitch." He simply sat there like that, head hung low.

"You okay?" Veles asked.

"No." The Marine half-lifted his head to look at Veles. "We live in a nightmare."

"Or a badass fantasy," a lance corporal standing at attention behind him, and to Shrina's right, offered.

"Shut up." The staff sergeant stood then, motioned to Veles with a 'get out of here' wave of his hand, and said, "Do stay out of sight. And try to stop them before anything like this happens again."

"You're letting them go?" the lance corporal asked.

"Again, shut your face. And... yes." He made eye contact again with Shrina, gave her a nod, and pulled a flask from his desk. "Go, before someone else intervenes and stops you. Because without you, I don't know that we stand much of a chance."

Her first thought was to wonder what sort of Marine would be so defeatist. Then again, they had just been attacked by vampires, seen the Pentagon fall, nearly, and seen proof of some sort of dragon connection to all of this, in the form of what she had become. If she was in his shoes instead of living it first hand, she might want to tuck tail and run, too.

"Thank you," she said, and followed Veles out of there.

Exiting the room with one of the Marines as an escort, Veles leaned over to Shrina and said, "I'll get you whatever support you need."

"And... you?"

"I'll be just fine."

"Find my old team, and prepare them for... me. What I've become." She clenched her fists, wondering what might have changed about him in the rebirth process, claws digging into her skin. "Tell them to gear up. It's time for a hunt."

3

TRENT, REMALD

Trent loved being close to Feras, even when her elbow was pressed into his neck, her other arm wrapped around his head in a chokehold. His grin probably annoyed her more than if he had been winning.

"Focus," she said, releasing him and pushing him away, hands up and ready for more sparring. "You let your guard down on the battlefield, you die."

"I wouldn't be up against you."

"You don't know that."

He frowned, lowering his guard. "Feras, if I had to fight you, I'd let you win."

She cleared the gap between them to slam an elbow into his sternum before sweeping out a leg and sending him to the floor. "Correction, you wouldn't 'let' me do anything. Not if you don't learn to better hold your own."

He groaned, pushing himself back to his feet. "I can't. Not against you."

"Trent, stop being a jackass," Merax said. Trent had nearly forgotten the man and his two remaining top Ajargons—Dolog and Wilnar—were watching. Ezail had been there at one point, but must have gone to train on her own, or maybe been grossed out by his flirting with her mother. The three men stood near the wall with swords and spears, framed by two stone columns. A domed ceiling overhead made the room feel smaller than it really was, but Merax said the dome was to give more room for throwing each other, or occasionally using powers in sparring. At the moment, they were focusing on simple hand-to-hand combat.

"You do realize you're insulting her, right?" Wilnar said with a chuckle, arms folded over his large chest. "Every time you hold back a punch, you're saying you don't believe she can take it."

Dolog grunted in what seemed like agreement.

"Even you?" Trent asked the generally silent man. Cracking his neck, Trent turned back to Feras and nodded. "Allow me to restore your honor."

"Shut up." She lunged again, but this time he imagined it wasn't her at all. Instead, he focused on the image he had burned into his mind of Ohklon. When he blocked the first punch and side-stepped her kick, he came in with a knee and then stepped into it so that he managed to grab her, spin, and slam her onto the floor.

"That's what I wanted," she said with a laugh, then arched her back and groaned.

"Damn, sorry, I—"

"Don't apologize for doing it right," Merax cut in. "You want me to get in there and throw her around instead?"

"You could try," Feras countered, already up and coming back in at Trent, the two going back and forth with strikes, each time the other side blocking and attempting counters that didn't land. Now that she knew he was committed, she wasn't holding back either.

Wilnar let out a sound similar to a whistle, then laughed when Feras landed a kick to Trent's leg that left him falling to one knee and being exposed to the punch that followed.

Shaking his head to clear it and get back in the game, Trent put up his fists to block in case more strikes were coming, but instead found a knee about to hit his face. He thrust his forearms out, caught it, and heaved his body forward to catch her off balance and bring her to the ground. When he was on top of her, pinning her in an arm bar, he couldn't help but notice her grin.

"Focus," he said, teasingly.

"Oh, I am." She rolled into it and wrapped a leg over his head, then kept rolling to toss him over and pull him into a triangle choke. "This is what the smile was for. Not whatever you were thinking."

He had to tap out. "You... you're badass."

"You're not so bad yourself."

"Earthers and their hang-ups with losing to females," Wilnar said, shaking his head with a chuckle. "Or… is that just you?"

"Far as I know, I'm not as bad as a lot of Earthers," Trent countered, giving Feras a nod of respect. She was hardcore, and had earned it.

"I guess when females sometimes are the largest dragons, that notion is squashed real fast." Merax stepped into the room, offering Trent his hand and then helping him to stand. "You're progressing fast, and I know for a fact you'll be useful on the field with or without the light."

"Thank you."

Merax grunted, then motioned to Wilnar and Dolog. "You two next. We all have to stay sharp."

Trent joined Feras at the edge of the training room, leaning against one of the stone pillars as he caught his breath. She eyed him with a grin that told him he wasn't the only one who had been enjoying their close contact, then nodded for him to take a walk with her. He went, after first taking a moment to linger at the doorway, watching as Dolog went up and under the taller man, managing a takedown that should have given him the advantage. However, Wilnar was fast, and seemed to have let the other man think he had the advantage, only to spin and bring him down into an ankle lock.

"Practice your riding," Merax said, seeing the two of

them leaving. "Much of our combat will be in the sky—can't have Trent falling off and dying on us."

"You've seen him in action," Feras said, but nodded. "But of course, we can always improve."

Merax grunted, watching as Dolog delivered three solid blows to Wilnar. No matter how hard they dished it out, they always had the baths to heal them after. As long as no body parts came off, and of course the baths couldn't heal death. Still, it wasn't like anyone there was trying to seriously hurt each other. It was all in the name of training.

"You want me to ride you?" Trent whispered when they were in the hall, and wrapped his arms around her neck. "Gladly."

She laughed, pressing her lips to his and then shoving him away. "We're training, as he said. Don't get the wrong idea."

"Hey, where I'm standing—"

"We can all see where you're standing." She glanced down, winked, and then kept on down the hall. "Keep up."

He frowned at her use of words, but then jogged to join her at the stairs to the sky door. As she led the way, he couldn't help but admire the gold armor and the way it clung so tightly to her curves, yet did such a great job with defense. When in relax mode, the armor transformed to simple robes. This world was a mystery to him, but one he rather enjoyed.

She reached the top, opened the door, and stepped

aside, giving him a knowing look. "We're supposed to be training, Trent. Get your mind where it should be."

"Is yours?"

"Not remotely, but I never expected to find romance again. It's not my fault."

He laughed. "And here I was thinking I was stranded, left for dead, before you came along. I can focus on pleasing you and fighting off Ohklon equally."

"Hmm." She winked again, then stepped out into the orange light.

The brightness caused him to blink so that he nearly missed her transformation. One moment she had the armor, then it was floating off of her, moving around her body like loose robes falling away, and then flying back to form wings of light. Another blink and her body was expanding, changing its form until she stood on that ledge as a large, golden dragon.

I accept, her words came into his head, and it took him a moment to realize what she was referring to— his promise to both fight Ohklon and please her with equal resolve. He grinned, then ran over and climbed onto her back, armor protecting him from her own scaly armor.

With a running start and flap of her wings, she plunged over the side. A gust of wind took them and they were up, soaring through the open sky and away from the city with its dragons circling—maybe guards on patrol, or maybe younger dragons simply having fun. Feras flew away from them and the temple and ice caves, leaving all of the politics and stress behind. Out toward the water, and the strange, spiked trees in the land beyond.

Not trees, Feras communicated. *More like the planet's way of telling us where we can and can't go.*

"I don't understand," he said, leaning into her, feeling the vibrations of her breathing, the muscles moving as she flapped her wings—even through his armor.

When the invasion comes, you will.

Seeing as she left it at that, he didn't press further, but stared at the area for a while before turning his attention to the water below. A large shape formed, and he realized it was the reflection of Feras. She had turned to veer right, soaring toward an island.

Sometimes, I like to go there to think, she told him. *Though, as you can imagine, it's not exclusive. With so many dragons about, it's hard to find anywhere to be truly alone for long.*

"We've made do, so far."

A warmth spread through her, along with a deep rumbling. Laughter?

To an extent.

It wasn't enough for her? Since their fun in the baths, the two had been taking every opportunity they had to move into dark corners to kiss, caress, and more. But it was true that they hadn't gone all the way, and he wondered at that. Maybe part of him was intimidated at the idea of making love to a dragon shifter? He knew she wasn't going to transform half-way through and bite his head off or anything like that, but there was definitely something holding him back.

No words could convey what he was feeling, though, since he couldn't quite put a finger on it to begin with. Instead, he simply ran his hand along her neck, enjoying the moment. The wind whipped his hair back, the fresh air filling him with the reminder that he wasn't home. Back on Earth, air never tasted so good.

"When this invasion comes," he started, "We'll be ready?"

If we can find those who have infiltrated our side, and eradicate them. If we can work together, harnessing the power of Remald, we might stand a chance.

"You're sure one for motivational speeches," he replied with a laugh. "Got me all fired up."

I speak the truth, as I hope you always will.

Another jab at his hesitancy, he wondered? A jolt went through him as Feras changed her trajectory, going straight down and then pulling up at the last second, causing water to spray out and create rainbows all around them. Not like the rainbows of Earth, as these met with the orange light that illuminated this planet, but similar and with more vibrancy.

Not everything is about sex.

"Can you not be in my head all of the time?" he protested.

I am only in your head when I'm in dragon form, she countered. *And in this case, it can't be helped. We are bonded, in that way.*

"Oh?" He found himself smiling, liking the idea of a

mental bond—not something he had ever shared with anyone. Though he wondered if that was similar to what Ohklon had come at him with, after taking his blood to escape the dragon carcass.

Very, very different.

He chuckled. "That's damn good to hear."

She flew up again, but they stayed fairly close to the water, circling the island. From here, he was able to look down and see the shore—black sand that led up into thick bush. Trees covered much of the island, those ones with large, purple leaves that jutted out in triangles, giving him the impression of a magnetized tile game he had played as a child. They drew close and an animal scurried across one of the leaves, moving over the edge and out of sight. From what he saw, it was furry with almost Dumbo-like ears.

A flock of what could pass for birds took to the sky, though as one flew past, Trent noted that they were more like a mixture of bats, but with hideous faces reminiscent of something out of the Alien movies. Hey, they had gotten part of it right, but not on the animals that were a threat. He hoped.

No, they're harmless, Feras assured him. *And actually make quite the delicacy. Care to try some?*

"Er, not at the moment."

Suit yourself. She glided for a moment longer, both simply enjoying being together, but as she circled again, she went rigid at the sight of a dragon in the distance. Large, silver, and flying along the outskirts of the royal city.

"You know him, I take it?" Trent asked.

I know everyone. But... have a history with him.

"Oh?" It hit him that he wasn't sure what had happened with Ezail's father, but before he got a chance to ask, Feras responded.

No, not like that. More like, he pursued me and I turned him down, and ever since he has given me the cold shoulder.

"And that's so bad?"

The cold shoulder can be, when it's from the Prince. The royal family has been nothing but a horn in my side.

"Don't you mean a thorn?"

No. Like a horn, you know? Jabbing into my side.

He couldn't help but laugh. "Sure, I guess. Where I come from, maybe since we don't have horns, the saying refers to a thorn—like on rose bushes."

Rose bushes? I'm not familiar. But if it's a saying, those thorns must be incredibly dangerous. Earth sounds intimidating.

Although he had nothing to say to that, the fact that he was thinking about the small thorns of roses in comparison to the massive horns these dragons had made her realize his thought. Another one of those rumbling laughs followed.

You all went for a fly without me? Ezail's voice sounded in his head, and Trent turned to see her in dragon form, approaching. Neither of them had noticed, their attention so focused on the silver dragon, or prince, apparently. Her dragon form was smaller than her mother's, but equally as intimidating.

Trent's first thought was that they did a lot without

her, but that wouldn't have come out right. He was really starting to think of her as a friend and maybe daughter figure, though he certainly didn't mean to push himself into the role of parent. If it happened naturally, she was amazing and he would embrace the situation with wide, open arms.

"Good to see you," he called out, though he imagined she could probably hear his thoughts if he had simply thought it.

Not to the same degree I can, Feras communicated. *And... that's sweet.*

"Oh, right." *Get out of my head!*

Until death do us part? She hesitated, then added, *Joking.*

Hello! Ezail circled them, going up and over, then around again. *Some conversation here I'm unaware of?*

Follow us, Feras replied, sent to both of them this time, and she dove down toward the island. *I'd rather the prince not see us, if he hasn't yet.*

Here we go, Ezail added, pulling up next to them.

Trent still had a hard time believing this was really happening—him riding on a dragon who happened to be the woman he had feelings for, her daughter flying next to them, orange light glinting off of her scales. He looked up at the clouds floating by, feeling a light rain starting to fall and spending a minute appreciating its cool touch against his cheeks and the way the clouds had a purple tint with a red lining. Back home it was said that every cloud had a silver lining, but the related saying didn't quite have the same effect with red, did it?

Feras glided along, circling back to her daughter, as the three of them descended to the island. They landed on the sand, not sinking in as he would have suspected. When he dismounted, he understood why. It was sand, but whether from many dragons landing over the years or some natural factor, it was packed tight and even had a glassy feel at points. dragon's fire might have led to that.

"I'm glad you enjoyed the ride," Feras said, and he looked up from the sand to see both of them had transformed back to their humanoid forms. He tried not to watch when Ezail was around, because the transformation inevitably led to seeing more skin than he felt comfortable seeing on anyone other than a love interest. He supposed that was why this culture was less shy regarding nudity, but he wasn't there yet.

"Mom told you about this place?" Ezail asked.

"Not all," Feras answered before he could.

"Well then…" Ezail motioned for them to follow, and took off running into the trees. "Follow me."

"What's happening?" Trent asked.

"Better do as she says," Feras replied with a wink, then ran after her daughter.

Trent chuckled, glancing around as if they were messing with him and he would find the punchline hovering nearby, but then realized they were gone, sprinting off on this island. With a silly grin, he ran after them.

Charging through trees and leaping over stones and logs, Trent was like a child again. He couldn't count the number of times he had gotten lost in his youth, running around with Chuck or Sophie in woods like these but incredibly larger. Valleys where he had built tree houses, spent nights trying to camp in makeshift tents, and the time they had thought there was a bear that turned out to be Chuck's older brother messing with them. All of it came flooding back and he was in the zone, feeling that youthful thrill for adventure. Only, now he was living it for real!

He let out a whoop, then laughed at himself. A footprint on the other side of a puddle showed him where the other two had gone, so he kept on, eyes piercing the darkness of the shade cast by the trees, to find them. Movement to his right caused him to have to climb over a berm, then he was running almost into both of them where they grabbed him and held him in place to stop him from falling into an opening in the ground that was filled with water. No, not filled, he realized as he leaned over it, still in the process of getting his footing.

What he was looking into was an opening to the water below the island.

"There's a whole network of caverns down there," Ezail said. "The children of our people come here to swim—"

"Which they aren't supposed to do," Feras pointed out.

"Right. I certainly never did." Ezail winked Trent's way.

"But they aren't here now?"

"They would be in school at this moment," Feras replied.

"Wilnar's children love this place." Ezail waved off the look from her mother. "Or so I hear."

"Wait, why aren't you in school?" Trent asked her.

"I'm fifteen." She smiled, as if that was clear.

"School here goes until fourteen," Feras explained. "From there, it's all about martial training or finding your calling in other forms. On your world it's different?"

"Depending on the country, but yes. Standard education goes up through to age twenty-two, ever since Global Command made it so. That's sixteen years of education, though some go for more and others opt for less. Certain occupations, for example, allow for stopping after twelve years, and you can test out whenever you choose, if you want to go military or some related specialty that serves the government."

Ezail stared at him, mouth open. Finally, she coughed and said, "Sixteen years of school? I can't imagine there's enough material to teach for that long."

He laughed. "It's debatable, but I'm sure there are more efficient ways."

"Anyway, this is what I wanted to show you." Ezail motioned to the water. "Shall we?"

Trent wasn't sure he wanted to jump into that dark, deep water at the moment, but certainly wasn't going to back down. Luckily for him, he didn't have to make the choice.

"Save it for next time," Feras said, eyes to the sky

through the foliage, where they could just make out the area by the temple. She didn't move.

"Feras?" Trent asked.

Her response came as a hand raised, a finger pointing. At least a dozen black ships were flying from the royal city toward the temple of Merax. The type that had taken Trent from there before, as prisoner.

Ezail growled, starting to glow bright. "This can't be good."

At once, both Feras and Ezail transformed. Trent ran and took his spot on Feras's back, and the three of them flew off to the temple, hoping to get there before the royal ships.

4

ESPINOZA, KRASTIAN

Wind crashed outside the cave, even though the storm wasn't upon them yet. All manner of debris was being thrown against the rocks, so that the team had to stay clear of the entrance to avoid being hit. Everyone grew uneasy as the storm intensified, eyes shifting between the entrance to the cave and that damn Goldie.

"Forget this," Ruan said, as she stormed over to the Goldie sinking her teeth into his neck. The Goldie shook as she drained the gold life force from him. Nobody moved to stop her, as it wasn't any different from what they had been doing up to now, it was just that this time she was much fiercer. After a moment, she stood with that golden glow taking over, then she deliberately punched the Goldie in the face. It didn't seem to do it much harm, but was likely very satisfying

"What are you going to do, beat him to death?" Ellins asked.

"This is just the start." Ruan knelt in front of the Goldie, eyes focused on it. "What are you holding back? I don't believe for a second you can't communicate with us, so spit it out."

The Goldie simply stared at her, with its eyeless face. Ruan cursed, slammed her fist into his face again, before turning and stomping off toward the far wall. There she stood, hands against the wall, head down, clearly trying to come up with another plan.

"Well, that's clearly not working," Marick said, "But I agree we have to do something."

Even as he spoke the words, the rattling of the cave grew stronger. Thuds shook the ground, and everyone shared looks of horror. The sandworms were attempting to break in.

"Maybe they won't communicate with us." Espinoza approached the Goldie, kneeling in front of it. "We've been thinking about this all wrong. These things are just weapons, and in our case, we need to load up."

Having said his piece, Espinoza leaned in and drank from the Goldie too. It was like sweet honey, warm, and filling him with ecstasy. He pulled back and the Goldie went semi-limp. Now it was Marick's turn, but Espinoza held up a hand.

"Step aside," Marick said.

"Wait! I have an idea…" Espinoza knelt again, this time staring into the face of the Goldie. That strange liquid substance just beneath the skin was moving slower now as there was less of it, after he and Ruan had 'milked' it. Espinoza had felt something as he stepped away from the Goldie. A sort of connection.

You in there? Espinoza asked mentally. It was more than a thought, but something he hadn't been able to do without the gold liquid inside of him. Now, he felt this ability to push, even sensed Ruan stiffening as he did so. It seemed that she sensed it too, maybe even heard it.

A moment of nothing but the chaos of thudding and winds howling followed, and he was about to give up when the Goldie shuddered.

Every one of you will die this day, the response came.

"Holy shit," Espinoza said. "It worked.

"Mind filling in the rest of us?" Kim asked.

"Hold on," Espinoza said, finger up, and connecting with the Goldie again as Ruan explained that he was communicating with it, mentally.

Why are you attacking us? Espinoza asked. *We're not your enemy.*

Of course you are.

I don't understand why you would think that.

The Goldie cocked its head, then suddenly lunged forward, mouth open and golden light flowing from Espinoza to it. Ruan and Marick were on it in a flash of movement, slamming it against the wall as Marick took his fill. All that was left of the Goldie was a husk and light movements, as if it had once been filled right up with fireflies but now only a few remained.

All... will... die. The message was clear, but conviction was weak. *You will not enslave us this time. Never again.*

A flicker, and the last of the gold light went out, leaving only the skin of the Goldie to crumple up against the wall.

"That was… pleasant," Ellins said, a look of disgust on her face.

"Dammit." Espinoza stared at the limp skin. "We were getting somewhere."

"That place you were getting to is called death," Marick countered.

"He's right," Ruan added. "We saved your ass."

Espinoza nodded, muttered his appreciation, and turned back to the entrance. "Still, we were making progress. You heard what it said?"

"We heard nothing," Franco offered.

"I did," Ruan said. "Slaves. It talked about us making them slaves… but that doesn't make any sense."

"None at all," Espinoza agreed. "What I saw on the other side of the portal, though… makes me wonder if there are people out there. A group like us, a group unlike the Goldies. A reason this place is set up so defensively."

"This could be it," Espinoza continued, looking at the glow on his hands. He was glad to see the Goldie hadn't taken it all. His gaze returned to Marick and Ruan. Their glows were almost as strong as that of the Goldie when at his prime. "We make our move against them."

"In this?" Ellins demanded, gesturing to the storm outside.

"We find the portals in the storm, right? We find them when the Goldies bring that shit. So what better situation to move on them? They bring us the gold, we take it."

"You been practicing that one?" Franco asked.

"Just came to me."

A couple of nervous chuckles.

"The three of us against that?" Marick strode over to the entrance, where the debris was piled up outside. A moment as Espinoza considered that Levin hadn't made it back. Losing people in a situation like this meant their chances of survival were falling fast.

"We can do it," Espinoza said," trying to sound hopeful.

"Can't say I'm looking forward to it."

Espinoza moved over to join him. "It's the move. The only move."

He turned to look at the others, everyone turning to Ellins. She was still the highest-ranking Marine there, after all.

"Way I see it," Ellins said. "Vamps shouldn't be the ones to have all the fun."

"You'd go into the storm?" Ruan asked, skeptical.

"Not likely. But… we can play our part."

"Meaning?" Espinoza asked. He wasn't trying to challenge the chain of command, and definitely didn't want to step on the toes of his new lover, if that's what she was. But they all had their strengths and weaknesses. He had only just become a vampire, but that was enough. In that short amount of time, he had come to know at least some of his own limitations.

Ellins wasn't answering, but stepped up next to them, hand up to shield her eyes from the dust of the storm out there. She turned, found her helmet, and donned it. Faceplate down, she stood, arms folded, and stared out at it.

Her voice was harsher through the suit. "They want us. Use that. We'll stay back, one of you here with us, and we'll see if we can find ourselves a new hostage to speak up."

"I'm not using anyone as bait," Espinoza countered.

"Don't think of it that way. We're not bait, we're part of the strategy. With Marick hanging back, we'll be more of an ambush than anything."

He was glad she hadn't pulled rank. Maybe up here, it really was starting to mean a little less than it used to, as Franco claimed.

Espinoza gave Marick a 'you take care of them' look before turning to assess Ruan. He hadn't had much of a chance to fight at her side, but knew she could handle herself. Would she put her neck out there to save him, if it came to it? That didn't have as solid an answer.

"I'd rather be out there," Marick countered.

"Arguably, we'll need the strongest of the vampires in here," Kim pointed out, earning a nod from Ellins. "And no offense, Espi, but you're newer to this vampire thing than Marick is. And Ruan..."

"We don't know you as well," Ellins finished.

Right to the point. She had verbalized Espinoza's exact worry, but everything they said made sense, so Ruan gave them a terse nod, walked up to his side as she readied herself, and said, "Someone going to give us cover fire?"

"When they're not at the cave, yes. When you think they are, assume that's time to circle back."

"Roger that," Espinoza said.

He wanted to turn back to her and then Kim, give them each kisses in case he never saw them again... but of course, that wouldn't do. Both had looks in their eyes that they were having the same thought, and that was enough.

Together, armed and armored up, Ruan and Espinoza stepped out into the storm. Crashing winds didn't do much against them in their armor, and they chose not to fly in case the wind should carry them off course. At least, for now. The bursts of gold continued, but seemed to be random, not controlled or aimed at them necessarily.

"Move right, I'll go left," Ruan shouted, and was already running off.

"We should stay together!" Espinoza countered.

A crackling voice on the comms said, "She's not coming through on the comms. I'm guessing out of earshot already."

Espinoza looked back to see Ellins at the cave, or at least, he guessed it was her since she was the one talking.

"Roger that, Gunny." He cursed, debated with

himself whether he should go after the vampire, but instead went with her plan. They wanted to try and work the enemy toward the cave, so seeing about flanking maneuvers made sense.

As clouds of sand and gusts of orange gases surrounded him, he lost all sight of the cave, but pushed on, hoping his sense of direction would get him back when the time came.

5

SHRINA, WASHINGON, D.C.

Anticipation filled Shrina as she stepped out of the bullet-proof SUV and into the dark parking lot where she had agreed to meet those who remained of her old team. Veles had been called back to take meetings in his function as Secretary of State, but had sent a couple of his personal guards with her, in case there was any trouble, and to be there to vouch for her.

First she noticed the two snipers, thanks to her ability to see in the dark. One on the ground, one on top of a building.

"Not the best start to a reunion," she called out.

Richards stepped forward from the warehouse on the right, his car likely parked behind or hidden nearby. "What should we expect, after finding the others as we did, you gone?"

"Was there a rescue mission?" she countered. "You find them dead, me gone. I'd think you would tear through that country, leaving no stone unturned until you found me."

He nodded. "Of course. Instead, we find you here, on American soil... looking like you do."

"Judging books by covers now?" She chuckled. "Well, guess what? This book is complicated as hell."

"You always have been." He stepped forward, waving his hand. Shrina noted that the snipers moved back, no longer sighting in on her, at least. "This is what you became... why? You were bitten?"

"Does it matter?"

"Help me understand."

She approached him, eyes darting around to ensure she was safe, a motion to those behind her to keep her escort back. This was about her and her old boss, for now. Making sure he knew she was on his side.

"They got to all of us. An ambush." Images of the attack assaulted her, of her fallen friends... of blood. "I was left for dead with them, but... returned. Awoke, I guess you could say—like this."

"And you have no idea why?"

"I do, actually. The dragon—we share some sort of connection. I think it's related to the super-soldier serum I got. Maybe it had a special gene in it, something that connected us? The other version might be... that we're connected in some other way."

He nodded, stroking his chin. "It's going to sit wrong with some people. Make them uneasy, but... We have you on our side. It would be a shame not to harness such a powerful weapon."

"My sentiments exactly." She thrust out her hand, and they shook. Very formal, his hesitancy still causing a bit of rigidity to the whole procedure, so she kept the focus on the mission. "First, we need to find them."

"My team—er, our team, can help there. We've been tracking their movements, preparing to make an assault, but needed to be sure we were ready."

"I'm here now," Shrina assured him. "We're ready."

"Come on, then. And bring your friends." He paused, about to turn, but added, "About Landon and Roy, I'm sorry."

"Me too."

They shared a moment of silence for their fallen comrades, then Shrina nodded and returned to her vehicle. She told the guards to follow the FBI vehicle, and waited for it to roll by.

"Are you sure you can trust them?" one of the men asked.

Shrina turned, keeping her eyes on the snipers, now pulling back, and shook her head. "I'm not sure who we can trust anymore. But we won't get anywhere without taking some chances."

"Roger that."

She eyed the man, then the woman, both in the front seats. The woman made eye contact in the rearview mirror, then looked away. During the drive over, Shrina had been so deep in thought about her sister and meeting back up with Richards, she hadn't even considered these two. As far as she knew, they were legit—they were with Veles after all. He had proven himself, what with the fight at the Pentagon and his role in getting her out here to find Alicia in the first place.

"How long have you two been with Secretary Veles?" she asked.

The woman glanced back again, this time holding her gaze. "Since shortly after his involvement in the downfall of New Origins."

"Ah." She nodded, remembering all she had heard about those days. Veles had come into the government thanks to his connections formed while playing his part in taking down the overpowered corporation and their privatized military. Same as her sister and Marick, along with some of their other super soldier friends... and Trent. Dammit, she hated that these discussions couldn't help but remind her of him.

Why did so many people put their desire for accomplishments above real relationships? Above connections and what could be perfect lives with soul mates. Not that she considered him a soul mate, but she sometimes wondered what might have been. The ones who got away had often made her feel that way, though, so she dismissed it as yet again remnants of her puberty-driven mind and obsession with old movies that had shaped her ideas about love and finding her prince.

At this point, she didn't give a damn about any of that... but that's not to say that she hadn't once upon a time. Those kinds of thoughts were hard to deprogram.

Finally, the car appeared. Then another. Apparently, Richards wasn't playing around. She understood his need for precaution, though. Reports had likely reached him of her resurgence, and the fact that she resembled a demon or dragon. News like that wouldn't sit well with everyone.

The SUV purred to life and rolled out, Shrina shifting uncomfortably to get her wings to fold at her sides and allow her to sit back. Someday, she would get used to her new look, she had no doubt. But that day was not today.

Looking down at the scales on her hands, a realization hit her. With all her thoughts of finding a prince and trying to get over Trent, she hadn't stopped to really consider what her new look meant in terms of someday settling down. Even though she had appreciated how handsome Trent was, she had never considered herself shallow in the slightest. But to expect anyone to accept her as she was, to love a woman with wings and scales... that was a bit much. Impossible, she thought, closing her eyes and focusing on her breathing, trying her best not to think about the loss of any potential children. All the dreams of a house in the suburbs, raising a family and maybe a cat... gone. Well, the cat might still work out. Even then, though, would any cat love her like this?

"Forget it," she muttered.

"What was that?" the woman at the wheel asked.

Shrina chuckled, hating her own self-pity. "Nothing." But it wasn't nothing. It was a moment for her, and a very important one. That point in life where she had to tell herself that none of her old dreams mattered. Not anymore. Not when there were vampires and a dragon-person out there to fight, and who knows what in space. The fact that some of the Marines had survived up there was really throwing her for a loop, along with the other implications. Especially in terms of this dragon business.

For her, there was little doubt that this dragon stuff had to be connected to all of that. Fantasy stories and magic were all make-believe fun to tell the kids at night. But she had always had a curiosity about space. Always wondered what other life forms might be out there, and how they would look. Her assumption had always been that they would appear more human than otherwise, because of old movies like *Stargate*, maybe. Or maybe it simply made sense to her, because she couldn't believe that Earth had never had contact with others in the universe, so had to think that the others would not be so incredibly different. Then again, it was entirely possible that life would be much more diverse, some would perhaps resemble Earth-dwellers, while other more extreme monsters might live in the distant reaches of the universe.

When she opened her eyes again, reminding herself that her purpose in life was bigger than all those other distractions now, she saw that they were pulling onto a freeway, heading toward Langley. Only, not two stops later, they took an exit and were making several turns in a residential district that she didn't recognize.

Of course, a safe house. She leaned forward, looking up at the large houses. Many were set back from the road and had large gates, often hidden by trees or tall hedges. Finally, they went through an alley between houses, turned up a private driveway, and into a three-car garage. All of the cars waited until the garage doors were closed before their inhabitants exited.

Shrina was last, very aware of the others with Richards, who seemed to be unable to help but gawk at her. She kept waiting for one of them to say something about her being a monster, a mutant or whatever other word they might choose, so that she would have an excuse to punch someone in the mouth. None did, and soon they had remembered themselves, turning to head in through a door at the top of the stairs.

Richards lingered, and Shrina motioned her guards to go ahead. He gave her a once over, then grinned, holding out his arm for her.

"Very professional," she said, not bothering to hide the sarcasm.

He grinned, not taking his arm away. "I figure you're going through a bit right now. Emotionally. Couldn't hurt to know you can lean on me."

"Oh, God." She rolled her eyes, but wrapped her arm through his anyway. "Just don't start singing."

He froze, and she blushed. There might have been a time where she had half-walked in on him in the bathroom before realizing she was in the wrong one, and he had been singing the "Lean on Me" song while piss-

ing. It was the only time she had ever known him
to sing.

At his glance her way, followed by a shake of his
head, he figured her out.

"Spying on me in the john?"

"Nothing like that, I promise."

"If you say so." He led her up the steps, past some
tables laid out with an array of food and to the open
doors beyond where the guards stood waiting. Shrina
eyed the food, and Richards gestured back to it. "Help
yourself, and feel free to bring it in. We've been
working around the clock, so people eat and catch
sleep whenever they can."

"That bad, huh?"

"Worse." He was about to go in, when he frowned,
eyes shifting.

"Spit it out."

"Just... nothing important. But, I wanted to say I'm
sorry. You know I didn't want you going out
there and—"

"This sounds like a fancy version of 'I told you so.'"

"It's meant to be an apology."

"No need for that."

He nodded, muttered a thanks, and entered the
room. The scent of fried chicken pulled at Shrina, and
she couldn't help herself. Hell, she was a demi-dragon
now, or a half alien being of some sort. What did it
matter if she took in a few thousand extra calories?
Adding a Sprite to the mix, she entered the room,
biting into the chicken as she followed the guards.

They all went to the table in the middle, where Richards had floating screens on display in a circle. Maps. Some global, some local. And several agents were indicating positions that then lit up red, staying that way while leaving a faded trail from where it seemed a similar spot had been before. Many of them, at least locally, were concentrated around D.C., but there were also groupings in Virginia.

"Wallops Flight Facility," Richards noted, seeing her looking.

She nodded. "I thought so. But why?"

"We think they're going to attempt another attack. Takeover, and try to fly out of here, like some of them did the first time."

That reminded her of the message from space. "And us?"

"Not *us* exactly, but... yes. The U.S. and Central are having a discussion..." He looked at Veles's people, but must have decided it was fine for them to be there, because he continued, "They're in talks about how best to get our people back."

"Back?" She frowned at the thought. "So the mission's cancelled?"

"At the moment, their primary concern is getting those Marines to safety."

"There's a reason they aren't safe up there?"

Richards looked from the maps to her, then to the others. "It's not something we should be discussing here."

Damn, so there was a reason to be worried. Shrina's

attention was piqued, but he was right that they needed
to focus on the vampires, the dragon, and her sister for
the time being.

"So that's our target then," Shrina said. "We move in
there, intercept the group, and hope the dragon is
among them."

Richards nodded, and just then looked past her
with a smile. "Ah, and your old friend is here. Agent
Chung."

Shrina turned, hoping he was joking. The woman
had gotten on Shrina's nerves, honestly, and was the
last person she wanted seeing her in her new state.
Like someone lying in the hospital in a gown and crippled, having a visit from their enemy who always
seemed to want to see them knocked down. It sucked.

Except, Chung was staring at Shrina like she had
just beheld the sunrise from Mt. Fuji for the first time.
After a couple of seconds of that, she ran forward,
stopped abruptly with her hand half out toward Shrina's wing, and said, "Can I?"

"Can you what?"

"Touch it. Your wing. I mean," she laughed, "sorry,
where are my manners." Taking Shrina in a hug, Chung
patted her back.

A tingling went up Shrina's back. "You did it, didn't
you? You touched my wing."

"Sorry. Dang. I mean… wow. WOW!"

"Agent Chung," Richards chided her with a scowl.

"Come on," Chung replied, gesturing at Shrina, then
taking one of her hands and looking at the claws,

running her fingers along the scales. "This is badass! Girl, you're the ultimate weapon now, right? I mean, I imagine you can kick some major ass like this, right?"

"Sure." Shrina pulled her hand back.

"And you're on our side, or you wouldn't be here. Going to go fight with us, get justice for our boys?"

"Yes."

"Exactly!" Chung held her hand up for a high five, but when Shrina didn't oblige her, moved on to the maps, going on about the way she saw the attack going down.

Shrina turned around, looking at Richards with an arched eyebrow.

"She's been a bit off ever since we picked her up, out there alone," he whispered. "She said she had thought it was over, left for dead. Turning over a new leaf."

"I'll say."

Shrina shrugged it off, turning back to the others who were starting to gear up.

"Come on, Drako, let's kill us some blood suckers," Chung said, winking as she walked past to go for her own gear.

"Don't call me that." Shrina followed, gearing up. She had a feeling this was going to be a long night.

6

TRENT, REMALD

S eeing the temple surrounded by the black ships made Trent feel very uneasy, his shoulders tensing as he held on to Feras. She had flown low to stay out of sight—as much as was possible out in the open like that—with Ezail keeping a bit of a distance behind her. Trent hadn't understood the need for such precaution, but when he questioned it, Feras had sent him the explanation, *With the royal guard, it's always better to be cautious.*

"How can we hope to fend off the Exiles when there's such a lack of trust between us on our side?" he asked.

It's because of the fight against them that these rifts exist. I agree, but... it is what it is.

Feras usually struck Trent as one of the wisest women he knew, but her dismissal of this issue struck him as way off. Her lack of a response to his thought now made him wonder even more. Instead of focusing on it, though, he turned his attention to the three men in black behind purple energy shields, all with their weapons pointed in their direction.

Standard practice for their kind, Feras explained. *Most of the guards aren't shifters—among the "Noshar"class. And therefore they've developed their own type of weaponry specifically geared toward fighting my kind.*

"But to be clear, they're enemies with the Nije, just like us, yeah?" Trent asked.

Except for those that the Nije have perverted, yes.

"Right, those." At least the men weren't firing, so he figured it was all defensive. Meaning they had likely arrived with someone of importance. Not the Prince, as they'd just seen him flying about the castle.

Worst case, it'll be...

The voice trailed off as Merax and a regal looking woman emerged from one of the lower levels of the temple. Her hair was up in a gray bun with glimmering purple jewels in it, a gown of purple and blue to match, with black cloth that rose up behind her in a way that reminded Trent of the spiked trees. As Feras came in to land, the woman's eyes narrowed, her gowns fluttering around her from the wind whipped up by Feras's wings.

While Trent expected more in the form of mental communication, none came. He had to assume this was the 'worst case' and that this woman wasn't exactly on the best of terms with Merax and the rest of the Ajargons.

"Your Majesty," Feras said, bowing at the waist. It

was all very medieval, which Trent assumed bore some relation to what she had told him before—about the connection to Earth and how some of their kind had found their way there long ago. Either they had influenced Earth culture or vice versa, but it was pretty amazing that such aspects of the culture still existed after all this time.

The queen, as was confirmed by the way Feras had addressed her, simply nodded, eyeing each of them in turn but with a special focus on Trent. She nodded to one of her guards, who stepped forward.

"Merax has taken full responsibility for your escape, but that doesn't mean you're off the hook." The guard, a tall man with wispy, black hair, grunted, holding out his hand with the blue light that had been used as restraints before on Trent. "I trust you will make this easy on all involved."

"You won't be taking either of them," Feras said.

"Don't," Merax started, but Feras stepped up to the queen, ignoring the way the guards stiffened, hands reaching for their weapons. Those who were already armed and prepared with shields exchanged nervous glances.

"You make this move now, we all lose." Feras turned from the queen to address the rest of them. "The exiles are returning, and likely already have some of their members among your ranks."

"Feras, Master of the Skies, I advise—" the guard started.

"She won't listen to a word you say," the queen

interrupted, running her hand along her gown to smooth it out, eyes still on Trent. "Kill her."

Trent stepped forward, hands up to show he was unarmed. "You can't—"

A blast hit him in the chest, purple meeting a shimmer of gold that had apparently acted as his shield. He stumbled back, confused by the idea that he had just been shot, and then turned to the female guard who had pulled the trigger. She was glaring, ready to do it again if need be.

But the act of her shooting had crossed the line, and in that instant Feras closed the distance between herself and the guard, snatched away the gun, and spun to hit her with wings of light that sent the woman to the ground whimpering. The gun went flying away while the rest of the guards turned their attention to her. It was all getting out of hand fast, but before Trent could figure out his next move, Ezail came swooping in, still in dragon form, landing on one of the ships behind the guards and using her tail to knock them into their own shields. A spate of shouts and curses followed, and then Merax had thrown off the men at his side and transformed at the same time as Feras did.

If Trent had blinked he would have missed it, but then the queen transformed in a flash and was a dragon too, purple with lines of silver. Guards scattered, Trent backing up as well.

"This is insane!" he shouted, realizing he held basically no sway here, but unable to sit back and watch them tear each other apart without at least speaking up. "You all are supposed to be on the same side! While your enemy hides in the hills and infiltrates your city, you argue about what? Me?" They all turned to him, not attacking, at least, so he continued. "This is over what? My blood being used by the enemy?"

"Or maybe by the queen herself, if she has her way," Dolog said. A man of little words, but when he used them, they were weighty.

"How dare you?" one of the queen's guards shouted angrily, aiming in on him now. Dolog and Wilnar stood at the same doorway that the queen and Merax had come through. Neither shifter had transformed yet, which certainly said something.

After a moment, the queen snarled, but then transformed back to herself, cloak floating around her as she did so. As the light formed back into her purple gown Trent couldn't help but notice her youthful, fit shape, despite the gray hair. She eyed him with a hint of curiosity mixed with scorn.

"The human is right," she said. "We won't do this. Not here. Not when our enemy threatens to burn our house from the inside."

At those words, the rest transformed back as well.

"What do you propose then?" Feras asked. "Because you're not taking anyone from the temple into your custody."

"First, let me remind you I am queen. Second," the queen strode over to her, each step bringing a thundering, mental attack to all, judging by the pain Trent felt and the looks of agony in the others. "Second, now that we all remember this fact… I will remember your place, and give you your dues. Indeed, I would like to extend an invitation. All are invited." She turned her gaze back to Trent. "Maybe we can have a private meeting of another sort, if I'm so inclined."

Having said her piece, the queen turned with a flurry of her gown, purple wings of light flashing out from her back momentarily, as she boarded the grandest of the ships. Trent wondered at the light wings. By his guess, they were activated when a shifter was close to transforming or right after, at times, and at others might be more related to emotion.

None of the temple dwellers moved until the rest of the guards were moving out, the one who Feras had attacked being helped away by two others. Finally, the ships took to the sky and departed—all but the one Ezail had landed on before, which was grounded.

"That could have gone better," Merax said, breaking the silence.

"Could have and should have," Feras added. "But there was no possible scenario that saw her leaving with the two of you. Not when we don't know who can be trusted in her ranks."

"Agreed," Wilnar said.

"She would have kept us under watch," Merax countered.

"Ah, but if a spy tried to poison you? Slit your throat in your sleep?" Wilnar shook his head, chuckling. "Bye bye boss man."

"Right." Merax rubbed his throat. "I don't suppose I thought through all the scenarios."

"You never do," Feras cut in.

"When the queen commands you come with her, you don't attack her guards." Merax laughed. "I can't imagine this will end well, but... won't lose hope, either."

"What happens next?" Trent asked.

"Hop on your lady friend there," Merax said, indicating Feras. "We're not turning down an invitation from the queen."

7

ESPINOZA, KRASTIAN

Out in the constantly changing moments of darkness with flashes of gold light, Espinoza had no idea how long he had been searching for signs of Goldies in the storm. He kept pushing through, trying to keep the direction of the cave in mind but backpeddling from time to time. When the Goldies came, he didn't want to have to face them completely alone.

Where had those bastards gone? Goldies had to be in this storm somewhere, no doubt about it. Now, his nerves were getting hold of him, anxiety rising at the fact that he was out in this bullshit storm without a damn thing to show for it.

A burst of gold light went off entirely too close and he fell back, blinking to get rid of the black spots in his eyes—even through the shading of the facemask, that had been a bit much. His next instinct was to bring his rifle around, but no follow-on attack came. With a curse, he was up and running left, a horrible thought hitting him.

What if they were waiting for the gold light to wear off?

If that had a remote chance of being true, he needed to amp this search up a notch. Forget the old strategy, it was time to pull them out of hiding.

"Come on, you sons of bitches!" he shouted and leaped up, flying into the air and letting out a four-round burst from his rifle.

Thrust off course by the wind, a second later his armor was pelted by one of his own bullets! How strong did that wind need to be for that to happen, he wondered, not wanting to know the answer.

A moment later though, he found his tactic had worked. Maybe they hadn't been waiting at all but simply didn't know where he was, or maybe one of theirs had lost its temper. Whatever the reason, a gold form nearly twice his size came pummeling into Espinoza, slamming him down to the ground and throwing his helmet off. Face moving close, it opened its horrific mouth and started to draw the gold energy out of him.

Espinoza wasn't going down without a fight. The Goldie clearly hadn't been briefed on their new skills, because when Espinoza managed to kick him off and then go flying sideways and up into the air, the Goldie merely turned as if taking him in, making note of it all.

Another burst of bullets tore out, a couple of them hitting their mark in spite of the wind, and then more rounds sounded from the cave. That got the Goldie's attention, though the bullets didn't connect. They hadn't accounted for that. Nor had Espinoza counted on the gold bolt like lightning that suddenly hit him in the back.

Excruciating pain shot through his spine and limbs as he was sent spiraling back to the ground. He landed with a thud, instantly able to push himself back to his feet as more energy than he could have imagined coursed through him, healing the sudden bursts of pain. Apparently, the bolt had brought energy, along with the damage.

But the Goldie was gone.

More shots came from the cave. Since the action was back there, Espinoza bolted off in that direction, three steps into it getting hit by more gold bursts and spasming in pain as he felt himself growing stronger and faster. He even seemed to be growing in size, so that when he was close to the cave and plowed into the Goldie in the sky, shots rang out. A barrage, tearing through the air all around him.

He thrust the Goldie off, easily overpowering it in this heightened golden state he was now in, and flew away to get clear of the shots. More rang out, coming in his direction. With a curse, he realized they were firing on him! As far as they knew, he was a Goldie. Looking down at himself, it wasn't hard to tell why. Hell, even his armor was glowing, the light starting to form what looked like flowing robes.

You aren't one of us, a voice said, and he spun to see a

Goldie on the ground, staying low with its face turned his way.

No, I'm better than you. He thrust himself at his enemy, facemask up so that he could plunge his teeth into the bastard's neck.

More power surged through him as he engulfed the energy of this being, more gold lightning striking. In the distance, too, he saw bursts of it. Ruan, perhaps. Somehow, with the gold energy already in them, the storm was attracted to them and lighting them up with more power. It started to give him a sense of how these Goldies worked, maybe. Portals in the storms, with them coming through and likely gaining some power from the storms themselves before attacking. Not unlike the Hulk with gamma rays, from those old comics, but this was some other energy altogether. At least, Espinoza hoped so! The idea of his body flowing with radiation didn't sit well with him.

One Goldie down, he noted as the being became a shriveled skin. Espinoza was hit by more fire, then static interspersed with, "Where… you…?" from Ellins and Franco.

"Stop firing at me!" he shouted back, though he didn't think it likely the message would fully make it through.

He decided he needed to get back there to check on them, but couldn't make a direct run on the cave or they would think they were under attack. So far, the bullets hadn't done much damage and he was feeling damn invincible with the power from the gold light.

That didn't mean he wanted to take the risk, though, especially when they might try hitting him with blasters or attempting other forms of attacks.

Going around to his left, he could see the cave in a haze of orange and black, and remembered to put the faceplate back down. That at least kept the dirt out, and allowed him to see his companions view through the HUD display. For some reason, the Goldies weren't showing on the display, and neither, actually, was Ruan. Too much interference, he imagined.

Comms cut back in as he got closer, and it was instantly clear there was trouble. Shouting, calling for him to get back. The grunts and clashes of some sort of struggle, along with a couple of shots. Damn.

He picked up the pace and saw the cave as Kim's voice came in, "Die you maggot-licking, shit stain!" A burst of shots, then the sizzling of a blaster cutting through something.

Espinoza reached the entrance as Marick's voice came through the comms as if from a great distance, telling someone, "I have him." And then they came into view, Franco and Kim with rifles and blasters, Ellins held to the ground by a Goldie that was sucking gold light from her while Marick tried to pull him back, teeth sunk deep into the being's neck.

"Another at your six," Ellins muttered, and they turned to fire.

Espinoza glanced back, only to realize they were talking about him. He dove right, held his hands up and said, "It's me!" through comms. "Friendly! Friendly!"

"Shit!" Franco cursed, pulling his finger off of the trigger, and then Espinoza shot past them, throwing himself between the Goldie and Ellins so that he was able to slam his forehead into its face, then pull off his helmet and sink his teeth into the opposite side of its neck from Marick.

A deep connection with Marick washed over him, as if the two had been best friends since birth. In that moment, he could see pieces of the man's life. Marick with a woman—the famed Alicia, almost certainly—in a kitchen overlooking a blue sky, both laughing and holding each other, the woman holding up a ring on her finger, looking at it as if for the first time. Shipping off, heading to a shuttle that would take him up into the sky, and then it was the takeoff. The space station came into view, New Origins clearly written on one of the tall buildings. Fighting, fiery explosions, and then Marick and Alicia, both looking much more weathered than in the vision of the kitchen, leaving a collapsing space station behind. Finally, the two in what looked like some Middle Eastern tearoom. Colorful cushions, tapestries on the walls and a fountain in the middle of the room with hanging plants above. Why was he seeing this? Espinoza tried to pull away from it, but the connection was solid, not releasing.

Then he saw why this last part of the vision was showing itself to him—the first flash of red in Alicia's eyes. Marick's hand going to his teeth, feeling the points. Everything going black.

Finally, the connection broke and Espinoza was

able to pull his teeth from the Goldie's neck, overcome with emotions at what Marick had just shown him, and more so with the knowledge that Marick had just experienced much of his life as well. The empty skin of the Goldie fell between them, Ellins groaning and rolling away. Marick and Espinoza, though, stood there staring at each other.

"Thank you," Marick said, eyes focused intently on his—looking up, because of Espinoza's enhanced size. "What... is this?"

"Effects of the storm." Espinoza gave him a nod, meaning to show him that he understood the man, and respected him. It was enough, so he turned to kneel at Ellins's side. "You're... okay?"

She nodded, letting him help her to stand. Looking up at him, she held a hand to her chest, controlling her breathing. "That was too close, and only one of them."

"Apparently, they can get in here," Franco stated the obvious. "How many of them are there?"

"Not sure, and Ruan... she took off."

"We need to get her, form a better strategy," Ellins said. "I say forget this, we go through the portals if we can find them. Fend for ourselves on the other side."

"Good plan." Marick started for the exit.

"Where are you going?" Espinoza asked.

"To power up, like you."

Nobody argued the value of that, and Marick was gone anyway, already charging out and leaping into the air as he did so.

"He's going to be okay?" Kim asked.

"Far as I know." Espinoza went to the exit, weapon at the ready, sighting through and looking for any signs of more Goldies, or portals. He made a note to get on Ruan later for running off like that. Marick was, as far as Espinoza knew, stronger than him. He had been at this vampire thing longer, and before that was one of the old school super soldiers.

"The storm did this?" Kim asked, at his side, hand on his arm. A spark went between them, warmth with the touch.

"Those lightning-like bolts. Hurt like a mother, but yeah."

Shouts of anguish came from outside, followed by the sky lighting up and a silhouette showing. Had to be Marick. Again it happened, but this time, two bolts hit him and he was closer—or maybe that was just him getting bigger? The third time a bolt hit him, Espinoza took in a sharp breath, because that last flash of light had revealed other forms in the sky.

"They're making a move on him," Ellins said at his other side, weapon drawn.

"Hold your fire," Espinoza said, shaking his head. "One of those might be Ruan."

"Damn this place to hell." Ellins took a moment, then said, "Get out there. Take them down and get to the portal."

"I'm not leaving you all unguarded."

"It's happened before and we were fine. Before, when you all went off—I think... And it's more of a guess than anything, but I think they have a limited number of those things. If the three of you are out there, their attention won't be on us here in the cave."

"Plus, there was something different about the Goldie when he came in here," Franco noted. "It was like he needed to pull that light from one of us, or he'd run out of breath. Like something in here doesn't let him have the energy he needs, but he can drain it from us."

Espinoza glanced around the cave walls, wondering about that. He wasn't affected in any way, which he thought might have been the case since he was so much in Goldie form at the moment.

"The first we brought in was very... calm," he pointed out.

"Maybe some sort of meditation that can keep the effect at bay?" Franco offered.

"Or maybe we're reaching," Ellins countered. "We all need to be ready for whatever, and hope for the best."

Another flash outside, and this time it looked bad. What he guessed to be Marick was grounded, three forms on him, another flying in from above.

"Go!" Ellins shouted, trying to shove Espinoza. It didn't do a damn thing, but drove the point home.

Leaving the others behind wasn't optimal, but he had a good number of the Goldies directly in front of him, at least where he could see them the closer he got. He hoped there weren't many more.

8

SHRINA, VIRGINIA

C hung hadn't stopped talking the whole ride over, recounting how her part of the mission in the hills had gone in the time leading up to Shrina's rebirth. At the end of it, as the vehicles stopped at their point of disembarkation, she leaned forward and said, "Think there's a way to make me like you?"

Shrina frowned. "You don't want that."

"Are you kidding? I'd give anything for this." She reached out and caressed one of the wings again.

"Stop it."

"Fine, but... is there? A way?"

Shrina noted that a couple of the others were glancing their way with looks of curiosity. Maybe they weren't giving her a hard time, but actually wished they could be like her. But they only saw it from the outside. They weren't considering the other time not spent fighting or hunting vampires. None of them were thinking of what it would mean for their families and friends.

Even if she didn't have a problem with spreading this curse, she wasn't sure how to. Bite them or feed them blood, all while hoping they didn't die, or would come back from the dead?

"I can't help you, not in that way." She grabbed her vest, realized she had no way of putting it on, what with her wings in the way, and instead only strapped on a thigh blaster, then grabbed an arc baton belt. Finally, she hefted up her DD4 assault rifle and turned to the doors, ready for action.

Piling out through the doors, they made their way up the hill that would lead to the lookout where their maps were showing the blips of the vampires.

Shrina was the one to lead the charge, running up and over the hill with her rifle at the ready. She saw the vampires below, and didn't hesitate. Throwing her arm out and wrapping it back around the sling to steady her rifle, she breathed in as the rifle rose up, and breathed out as the rifle lowered. Squeezing the trigger she let off a four-round burst. Two vampires fell to the ground.

Then she was charging again, as more shots rang out around her and to the rear. The rest of the groups were approaching, starting their assault. She meant to get in there, to find her sister, if Alicia was here at all. To find the dragon.

A vampire charged at her but fell as it got caught up in the cross-fire and shots hit it in the head, then another one turned and saw her but this one, she took out on her own. Rifle still up at the ready, she shot at point-blank range so that the vile creature's head exploded. Then she spun and drew her blaster with her other hand, finding that her increased powers gave her more focus. When the next vampire charged, she used it to kick off so that she went leaping into the air with her wings outspread. One good flap and she was up, blasting at the vampires that were now coming at her from all angles. Then she thought she saw Alicia. Wings back so that she could dive in, Shrina was back on the ground, unleashing more shots at anything that moved.

Two shots hit her on the shoulder and abs, sending her stumbling backward. Both wounds started healing instantly, but that didn't mean the pain went away. Gritting her teeth in frustration, she pushed forward, rifle butt slamming into heads, her blaster cutting a swathe through her opponents, she was a killing machine. Of course, these vampires didn't die like normal people would. Some dropped dead. Others fell, but she knew they would get back up when they'd had time to heal. In a way that made her feel better, because she knew that, on some level, even these vampires didn't really know what they were doing. They were under the influence of the dragon, or at least brainwashed in some sense.

She spun, eyes searching through the crowds for any sight of her sister, but there was none.

"Alicia!" Shrina shouted.

Growls sounded, a circle of vampires closing in on her, but Shrina didn't care. She threw herself at them. Nearby shots rang out and then Richards was there, Chung charging up beside him, and they took out one side of the circle while Shrina went for the other. She took down three of the vampires with her bare hands, after re-slinging her rifle and holstering her blaster. In a sense, she enjoyed the thrill of the fight with close hand combat, using her claws as batons. She would fly up, then fling herself down on top of her opponents, bringing utter destruction. If her sister was anywhere out there, she would find her by sheer number of casualties along the way.

Again she shouted for her sister, but heard no response.

"Where's the dragon?" Richards asked.

"I'm trying." Shrina didn't bother with another response or question, but ran forward and leapt into the air again. Her wings took her up, up, farther and farther until she had a good vantage point to look down upon the rest of the fighting. There was no sign of the son of a bitch.

Rage boiled up inside of her, the scent of blood filled her with longing, and she understood where the vampires were coming from. Only in her case, it was the blood of these vampires that she craved. It was vengeance. Justice.

If the dragon wasn't there, and therefore no Alicia either, then she had no need for these others. What happened next was out of her control, pure animal rage boiling up inside her, and unleashing through her fists, elbows, claws, horns and arc baton. At one point she had her blaster out, or her rifle, while at other times they were slung again or holstered, and she was biting, thrusting, clawing, ripping open flesh, stomachs and unleashing their innards onto the ground before them. It was utter destruction. Sometimes she would regain her composure and simply do her best to knock them unconscious, but mostly she wanted this done. She needed to move on, because her sister was out there somewhere, under the control of the dragon, and she needed to be rescued. Maybe not rescued but... set free?

Then there came a moment when she could only see two more left standing. Shrina charged at them, grabbed each of their heads and slammed them together. There was a sickening crunch and both slumped to the ground. Shrina stood there wiping the blood off her hands, staring out at the trees as they typically swayed with a light wind. She watched as a bird circled far in the distance and took off, likely startled by all the chaos. Any that would've been closer were long gone.

Another sensation pulled at Shrina, causing her to spin, eyeing the fallen vampires. One was crawling toward her, eyes fading in and out of red. Dark skin, hair matted down with blood. Shrina took a step toward her, wondering what this vampire's goal was at trying to reach her in that state, but then froze. She knew this woman.

"Trish?" Shrina ran to her, kneeling and holding the vampire's face even as the woman tried to claw at her. The red faded again, and those eyes focused on Shrina's.

"It really is you."

"How...?" Shrina shook her head, confused, but then realized it all made sense. Trish had come down with the other super soldiers, along with Pete. If Marick and Alicia had turned vampire, it only followed that this woman would have, too.

Again, Trish's eyes went red and she tried to push herself up to attack, but Shrina held her there. There was no reason to believe she could change this woman, other than a desire and a feeling. Clinging to that, Shrina willed her old friend to break the bond with the dragon, to be free of the madness.

It worked!

Not only did the red instantly fade, but Shrina felt a connection to Trish, as if a bond had been tied between them. An awareness came over her as she sensed first Trish, then several others nearby, all coming into her sphere of influence.

You are with me, Shrina pushed out. *Stand.*

Indeed, they did as commanded. First Trish, pushing herself to her feet in spite of her wounds, then the others nearby. All within what seemed to be about a twenty-foot radius of where Shrina knelt. Some fled, but a few looked to her, confused, seemingly waiting for orders.

"Shit!" someone said, turning with gun at the ready.

"No!" Shrina shouted, hand up to stop them. "They're with us, now."

"Explain yourself." It was Richards, kneeling with a smoking wound in his shoulder, a bit off to her left. He, too, pushed himself up, staggering over and eyeing the vampires. None moved to attack, their eyes on Shrina for their orders. "You're not making sense."

"I've taken them," she explained. It was the only way she could understand it. Somehow, maybe due to their weakened state or simply their proximity to her, she had taken control of them from the dragon and made them her own.

Richards blinked, looked at her and then the vampires, and simply nodded. "Good. Fine. Get me a medic."

He started to fall, but Shrina was there to catch him, calling out for a medic. Others rushed over and took him, explaining that they would get him to a hospital. They weren't on an official battlefield, and didn't have a medic with them, a point that Shrina found incredibly ironic, considering this was the new battlefield. In the near future, she had a feeling there would be a lot of cities and surrounding areas becoming such battlefields as this.

"They're coming with us," she explained to a stunned Chung, leading her newly acquired vampires to the vehicles. "Actually..." Pausing, Shrina looked back over the rest of the fallen, and searched with a mental push. Two more groaned, pushing their heads up. No red in the eyes. They were starting to heal, she saw as skin formed over a wound on one of them. Somehow, her connection to them was helping to speed up the process.

As those two joined the others, Trish staggered up to Shrina's side.

"It's good to see you again," Shrina said. "I only wish it could have been under different circumstances."

"Pete," Trish said. "My brother… he's still out there."

"For now." Shrina gave her a nod. They would find him and Alicia. And now that she knew she could 'recruit' some to her side, her confidence in the matter was soaring.

9

TRENT, REMALD

Nothing about flying into the city of the queen who had recently ordered him to be arrested and almost got into a dragon fight with his friends felt right to Trent. The alternative, however, was far worse. They needed to cement this bond, or they could find themselves fighting a war on two, or even three, fronts.

"I'm not sure what exactly to expect here," Trent said, clinging tight to the back of Feras as they approached the royal city.

Be yourself. Friendly, but ready for anything. You're the approachable stranger, cocky and not about to take any shit from anyone, but also the one to calm us all down, if necessary. And if possible.

"Great."

They flew on for a moment, the city with lights in streams forming their own sort of column, spires, and a great arena he hadn't seen before right in the center.

All roads had a way of leading to it, and now that he noticed, the lights also formed a pattern that placed this arena in almost a deferential place.

Kept pristine to remind us who we aren't, Feras communicated.

"What do you mean?"

Exiles. When they weren't that, but were known by another name. The Apophian.

It took Trent a moment, but he had studied enough to know there was something to that name. "As in, Apophis, or Apep? The enemy of Ra, kind of. Serpent god...?" He laughed. "That makes a lot of sense, actually."

I'm not aware of Earth mythology, but yes, it might be that the name continued there, in an altered form. The Apophian is a word we don't use. Not anymore. They promoted a culture of warfare, of the strongest and most vicious rising to the top. We keep the arena to remind us all that we are not them.

Ezail flew up alongside them, adding, *The Exiles are gone.*

For now, Feras noted. *We must do all in our power to keep it that way.*

People were looking up from where they were seemingly attending some sort of religious ceremony, as Trent guessed by the way the front row was kneeling. He wanted to look into that at some point, to learn more of the ways of these people, but for now saw they were circling the palace, soon to be attending their appointment with the queen.

Ever wish you were home, back on Earth? Feras asked, flapping her wings to descend into the courtyard. *Do you think about your old friends and family, dream of finding a way off this planet to reconnect with your friends and family?*

He considered the question, eyes on a large mural decorating the side of the castle. This part of the palace wasn't like what he had seen earlier. Here he saw sharp angles and roofs that curved up at the edges. Gleaming purple and blue lines hinted at defensive tech standing by. That, at least, put him slightly more at ease.

"No."

As simple as that? Just... no?

"My home is here now, with you." He held tight as she touched down, and in an instant she was herself, turning to caress his cheek and kiss him, before stepping back as her robes became golden space armor.

At his look of curiosity, she glanced down at the outfit and said, "In the royal court, while robes would be more appropriate..."

"My mother means to send a message," Ezail said, stepping up beside them and also in her armor.

"Wouldn't it best to not to fan the flames?" Trent asked.

Feras gave him a look that said he didn't need to speak the obvious, while Merax and the others came in for landing. She advanced towards the large, black doors—angled in such a way that they reminded Trent of dragon wings.

"There are levels for trust," Ezail explained, stepping up next to Trent. "The Exiles were, of course, at the bottom. Others fill in the spectrum on various sides, and for my mother, the royal family has never risen up above, say, the halfway point."

"The Queen comes from the old guard," Feras interjected, pausing with the door partially open. "Meaning, she was one of them, once."

Trent didn't need to ask whether 'one of them' meant the queen had been one of these Apophian—what were now called the Exiles. That was clear. What he wasn't sure about was how that would affect their meeting that was about to happen, or whether any past connections to this group meant current affiliations. Even if the royal family had been connected, he had to assume they were in power because they had played a role in ousting the old regime. If there were insiders working to bring back the Exiles, the queen wouldn't likely be involved, when she had enough power to do as she wished.

Then again, he hadn't known Feras to be rash in her judgment of others, so chose to enter this meeting with skepticism and a defensive wall up. Inside, it wasn't the grand hall he had expected, but a room lit entirely by four fireplaces. Each fireplace contained a large stone that was ablaze, all black but with hints of red, blue, purple, and green. He stared at those first, before letting his eyes wander to the rest of the room. Metallic artifacts lined one wall, along with a small dragon's skull that seemed to have been gilded. Maps of star systems, paintings of great battles—both hand-to-hand and between starships. It was the sort of place he could spend hours in and likely still find something new to capture his attention.

"Please, enter," the queen said, walking past them through the wide doors and approaching the far side to stand by the fireplace with the purple stone.

Trent and the others continued in, and he followed Feras's lead, sitting cross-legged on the floor. As he did so he realized it was made all of stone, which made sense when considering the nature of these people. Fire breathers wouldn't likely stay in wooden homes. The queen remained standing, even as Merax and several of her guards entered to sit. Apparently, this was their way. Nobody spoke, all staring into the fire.

Trent lost himself in those flames, remembering a time when he was younger, when he and his friends had no worries. Sitting and roasting marshmallows, sharing a beer one of them had managed to steal from their parents. Nothing special about the memory, except that it was a simpler time. He was glad to have left those times behind—all of this was so much more fun.

Finally, another figure entered. Trent glanced up to see silver armor, black hair mixed with silver strands tied back. A man of great importance, a man who knew his place was above that of many others. The Prince.

"It looks like we're all going to be working together in the near future," the prince said.

"Your highness," Merax said, bowing his head.

"Thank you, Merax." He eyed the rest of the group, then stopped with his gaze on Feras.

"Why are we here?" Feras asked, staring at him, defiantly.

"The exiles have been growing closer to return," the prince said. "They have people in the hills, in the city. Before long, the war will return to our soil. We mean to ensure our side wins, even if that means having to work with the likes of you."

Before she could respond, an explosion rocked the palace.

10

ESPINOZA, KRASTIAN

Feet pounding for a few paces, Espinoza had lifted his rifle as he ran, but waited until he was close enough. Clearing the area around the cave, he leaped into the sky, propelling himself toward the enemy.

Only, it went dark. Not just the area where Marick had been with the Goldies, but everywhere around him. Spinning, he scoured the darkness for anything he could kick off from, not finding even a sign of the ground. A shout back to the cave brought nothing. Not even static.

Dropping back to the ground made sense, but he couldn't find it. A thought hit him—interference. Throwing up his face mask, he was able to see the storm again, the dust and bursts of light. Something in the storm had not only caused his HUD to go out, but the whole display to cloud over. Now he had to squint to see, all manner of debris flying through the air.

Even now he was able to see again he couldn't find the fight. In that short amount of time, he had gotten so disoriented he couldn't find Marick or truly know which direction the cave was in.

"Marick!" he shouted into the wind, but without reward.

Staying put wasn't getting him anywhere, and in fact the ground started rumbling. He leaped back into the air in the nick of time, because just then a sand-worm came flying out, leaping up and nearly catching his heel in its nasty maw. He had gotten so caught up in the idea of taking out those Goldies, he had nearly forgotten about the sandworms. On a plus note, he was pretty sure that all the action out here was keeping the enemy away from the caves.

He flew through the air, trying to get his bearings, looking for any sign of the fight or the way he had come, trying to stay close to the ground as he safely could while keeping an eye out for the sandworms. Darkness in the clouds, moving. Massive, so that at first he thought it was simply more clouds, then he realized it was a much larger sandworm—likely the largest he had seen yet.

Two other worms moved aside to give way to the massive one suddenly in front of him, leaping his way, and he had to swerve left out of its path. Cloud cover gave way to a rocky cliff face, and he had to correct course to avoid slamming into it. A jolt like a magnet pushing him away hit from above and to the left, so he decided to investigate. Pushing up and away from the sandworms, he flew between flurries of orange and gold, then emerged to find a small cave there, partially obstructed by stones that seemed to have fallen long ago.

Gusts of wind hit the stones, but they didn't budge. The push was coming from there, but at least the stones appeared stable enough. He flew in, letting curiosity and a need to get away from those damn sandworms win out.

"This is a warning," he called out, rifle at the ready as he landed on the rock, ducking in and away from the storm.

While it was dark within, his golden glow provided enough light to see by. As caves go it was small, and narrowed as it went back. The hole at the end curved steeply downward, possibly an endless drop, although he had no way of knowing. Hopefully no bugs or strange animals would come scurrying out of there. Back on Earth there were leeches, ticks with Lyme Disease, and all manner of other nasty creatures that might lurk in a cave. Espinoza shuddered as his imagination led him to wonder what could be living in these hills.

No people, and no Goldies. What he did find of interest, though, was a glowing, golden rock, just where the hole curved in. So faint that, but for his newfound power, it wouldn't have even been noticeable in the dark. Maybe it was nothing, but he wondered, so he put a hand out to touch it. The closer his hand got, he realized, a wisp of gold light started flowing toward the stone and away from him. It glowed brighter then. He pulled his hand away, frowning. His power could fuel whatever sort of stone this was? Interesting, but he didn't know how it might affect him. Taking a step away from it, he held his hand up to the walls and noticed something else. A long, curved object that stood out from the rocks. Maybe white, but hard to tell in the gold light.

A bone?

The closer he got, the stronger the magnetic repulsion-effect held his hand at bay. When he was almost touching it, he was overcome with the urge to vomit, then stepped back, gasping for breath. He had no idea what sort of bone could do that to a person, but knew getting out of there was probably the smart move. No need to fight one of those Goldies in a place that would cripple him.

He turned to go, then froze at the sight of a Goldie hovering outside the cave entrance. The being's robes slapped about in the wind, but its wearer stood resolute. Without a doubt, it knew Espinoza was in there and was waiting for his departure.

Either the being was similarly affected by the large bone, or the Goldies had some sort of deference toward these caves. It was possible the cave Ellins and the others were in had a similar value or defensive status, though they hadn't known.

Well, if the bastard didn't want to enter the cave, Espinoza figured he might take his chances by insisting the guy join him. Stepping out as if to leave, he watched the Goldie lunge, then pulled back while at the same time, grabbing the being and pulling it toward himself. Probably the last thing the Goldie expected, and it showed.

A second later they were both in the cave, the Goldie spasming, part of it going limp, and then clawing for the exit. Espinoza caught up with it, first, grabbing the thing by the head and sinking his teeth into its neck. Energy flowed into Espinoza, but he didn't want to just feed on the thing, he had questions.

Where are the rest? He demanded. *How many are there?*

This... place... is forbidden! The response surprised Espinoza, who thought he would have to work harder to get anything.

Why?

Let me, leave. I can't stay here, I... The Goldie shuddered. *The old one—we do not belong.*

Explain. Pushing the Goldie toward the bone, Espinoza was intrigued to see that the being started shaking like he was about to explode. He pulled him away from it. *The others? How many?*

Five left, I believe. The being went rigid, its cloaks no longer flowing, a semblance of an actual face showing as if looking out from far away. *You should go home.*

So should you.

With that, Espinoza finished him off with one more drink, and then tossed him at the bone on the wall. Instead of blowing or melting as he had expected of the being, the Goldie went stiff like he had been suddenly frozen, then fell apart and scattered. Streaming pieces of gold rock, almost.

Whatever had caused that, Espinoza knew couldn't be good. And he didn't want to find out what it would do to him if he stayed around too long, considering how much of the gold power he had absorbed.

"Thanks," he muttered to the gold remains, then turned and launched himself back into the storm, going higher this time, in hopes of rising above it to get a better view.

Only, his flight was shaky and had less of a push behind it, leading him to fall partially. He regained his position in the air, floating for a moment while considering how lucky he was that the sandworms were gone, and then turned to look out at the night. Rumbling in the ground from his right, and if he was right about the sandworms—that they were attracted to action, but even more so to action when the gold light was involved—that's where he needed to be.

And along the way, he figured, gritting his teeth as he braced for impact, he could power up. Sure enough, flying through the clouds and toward the sound of rumbling in the ground, he saw a burst of gold ahead. Another, further up and to the right. Considering that there might be a pattern to the blasts, he shot forward and to the left, expending more energy than he would have liked, but instantly getting it back and then some as two bolts hit at once. The sensation was like old torture devices trying to rip his limbs from his torso, but the rapid healing and surge of power that came after made the pain worth the reward.

Then he was moving through the sky in a flash, gold fueling his sight to make out the forms still fighting ahead and in the sky. He drew close, rifle ready, and made out which were Goldies and which was Marick.

When one was clear of Marick, Espinoza squeezed the trigger. At least one shot hit, and then he was on the guy, firing at point blank range. Gold bursts of light showed shots hitting, though the being could heal fast enough that it wouldn't matter in the long term. Espinoza didn't plan on letting it get to that.

As fast as he had shot, he slung the rifle back so that it magnetized to his rear, then he had the Goldie in his grip, using his weight and will to throw them to the ground. Faceplate up, he went in for the bite.

It had almost been enough. Before he could sink his teeth in, though, the Goldie had its hands on him and shot out with a blast of energy that sent Espinoza rolling across the ground. He landed on his back in time to see the Goldie and another pouncing, both starting to pull on his energy.

Gold light streamed from his face in a way that tore at his soul, like someone pulling at your skin until the connecting tissues separate, then dug deeper. His shout of pain was swallowed up by the wind, but he wasn't without hope. Having been hit several times by those gold bolts of energy, he was damn strong. Plus, neither of the Goldies had bothered to keep his arms down or go for the blaster—likely figuring they would take him out fast or not understanding that the blaster was a threat.

Maybe not, but it could at least serve as a distraction.

Drawing his blaster as he struggled to maintain his bearing during all that pain, he managed to arch his back and get the position needed. A series of blasts caused one of the Goldies to jolt sideways. That was all Espinoza needed to be able to thrust up with his hips and get an arm around the other, bringing him in. Teeth breaking into flesh, he began imbibing the sweet nectar of these gods. With his enhanced power, it was one quick inhalation, and the Goldie was nothing more than skin, flapping until he let go so that the wind could carry the empty husk away.

Hesitation showed in the way the other Goldie moved back, then it was up and retreating. Only, as its portal appeared, so did Ruan. She flung herself into it, the two rotating through the sky with robes flapping about, behind them Marick having taken down one Goldie it seemed, but two more still on him.

Espinoza opted for helping Marick, as he was outnumbered. A well-aimed jump and he flew up behind one of the Goldies, hitting it with two blasts and then sinking his teeth into its neck. The being never had a chance, skin flapping away and out of sight.

Flying above, Marick and his remaining opponent were battling, but at a shrill sound, it retreated through the portal. One second later, the Goldie with Ruan attempted the same, but she caught it, draining it the whole way to the portal until, hand reaching out, it was gone.

She, however, didn't stop her trajectory. Without even a look back, she dove through and was gone. Winds still howling, swirling around the two vampires, they shared a look of frustration, each looking from portal to cave and back to each other again.

"Go!" Marick shouted, indicating the portal. "We can't leave her alone in there. I'll get the others and try to follow."

With a grunt to show he didn't like it but agreed, Espinoza took off, three heavy steps and then leaped into the air to fly through the portal after Ruan.

11

SHRINA, VIRGINIA

Shrina hated that she had to go back to headquarters, or the safe house anyway, instead of getting on with the job. She wanted to just charge out there, to find the dragon and be done with it. But there were too many other leads, too many places the vampires could be.

So there she was, standing with her new recruits, listening to Richards give his motivational speech to the agents. He wore a healing patch, and with his super-soldier enhancements, was seemingly healing well enough. Chung was rubbing her hands together excitedly, as if she had single-handedly taken on the vampires instead of Shrina. Everyone there knew who had really won the day.

Still, Richards congratulated each of them in turn, then selected some of them to go take some rest, to relax and take the night off, while others he picked out to form the nucleus of a team. This team would then go figure out the next steps to take.

When it was over, Richards approached Shrina, and said to her, "You have your own special team then. Make good use of them."

Shrina glanced back at her new recruits, and nodded. "They'll serve me better than a bunch of... non-vamps."

"Non-vamps?" Richards chuckled. "There used to be a time when that was called normal."

"Those days are gone... for now."

He nodded, then turned to go. "Chung will give you directions to the hotel. A spot to hang tight, lie low while we wait for the next steps."

"Roger that."

Chung meandered over, eyeing her skeptically. She held out her wrist device pointed up at a holoscreen, and then swiped over to pass on the instructions to Shrina.

"I'd be happy to help, any way I can." Chung waited, dismissing the holoscreen and eyeing Shrina with hopeful, childish eyes.

"This team comes with special requirements."

Chung nodded. "I'd be happy to take on those--"

"Stop right there." Shrina wasn't hearing any talk on people becoming vampires. Not from her, not from anyone.

She turned, going back to the team, and told them what was going on. For now, they didn't waste any time getting to know each other further or making small talk. They had their mission. And Shrina wasn't in the mood. She'd got her hopes up about finding her sister and the dragon, and right now she needed to move.

Soon they were back at the hotel, everything already being taken care of, checked in and all that.

That night, Shrina's sleep was a strange one, fueled by her connection to the other vampires. Even in her dreams, she was able to sense them, to even be aware of what the two on watch were seeing. If anyone attacked, she would be up in an instant, ready.

But there was more. A calling in the form of her sister's voice.

"He only wants us to return to him," Alicia said, voice carrying like a flute on a summer's breeze. "Together, the three of us. Come."

"Where are you?" Shrina asked. No response came. For a long time, she lay there, staring at the ceiling, repeating the question. Sometimes out loud, sometimes only in her head. Finally, she got up and went to the window of the hotel, just outside D.C. on the border of Virginia, to be ready for whichever direction they would need to go. She watched the headlights of a car driving in the distance, then turned her attention to the waning moon, the black and silver clouds.

Part of her wanted to be out there, flying, simply soaring over it all and ignoring her problems. But she was part of a team, now. Her sister needed her. This time, it wasn't like they had Alicia though, it was like Alicia's mind had gone over. Shrina wondered if she would be able to pull her back as she had Trish and the other vampires, or if this was more complicated.

How much simpler it had been when Alicia had been the one to always look after Shrina. She missed those days. Missed having a big sister to take some of the load off, to stand up to that jerk Trista in the schoolyard, back when the biggest problems of the day were some girl spitting on you, pulling your hair, and calling you a whore. All for eyeing a guy, who in all fairness had winked at her first.

Shrina grinned, humored by the way that still got her riled up. Trista was probably off working as a nurse or whatever, that same jackass—whose name Shrina couldn't even remember—off cheating on her. Fighting for what's yours made sense, but only when worth fighting for. That guy… not so much.

This clearly wasn't the way to get back to sleep, and Shrina knew she needed rest. So she dropped down for some sets of pushups and sit-ups, only her wings got in the way for the latter. Instead, she popped up and did some shadow boxing, using the vanity mirror to check her form and watch her movement. She was now faster than she could have ever dreamed, but awkward in the way her wings caught the air when trying to move. She needed to learn how to best use those, to leverage them in fights like this.

So far, she'd done a damn fine job. But she would go up against the dragon, eventually, and had to be ready.

The idea of a warm shower felt right, so soon she'd stripped from the day's uniform, chuckling at the fact that she had fallen asleep in it, and went to the bathroom. She turned on the hot water and then paused in front of the mirror while she waited, looking over her shoulder at the way her wings protruded from her shoulder blades. Just on the inside, actually. Scaly, bumps that she couldn't imagine anyone ever finding attractive. She was a monster... but a badass one at that. One who would use her monstrous badassery to bring Cody and the others with him down. To defeat the dragon.

As she turned, she noticed that her abs were looking more defined than before. Arms, too, and even her breasts were perkier. This whole transformation hadn't been completely for the worse, but then again, she wasn't sure it mattered. Self-confidence in terms of tight abs was a weird thing when also talking in conjunction with scales and wings.

She turned away and went to the now-steaming water, stepping in and lowering her head to let it wash over her. It was already hotter than she was used to, but she turned it up even more, then to all the way. Steam rose up, filling the shower and then the bathroom, until she couldn't even see her scaly hand in front of her face. The heat felt great, the inability to see her mutations even better. For a long time, she simply stood in that hot water and let it cleanse all of the negativity away.

From that moment forward, she told herself as she finally reached for the soap and began lathering herself up, those negative thoughts were gone. She was a demi-dragon with a purpose. A badass, sexy as hell demi-dragon. So what if she had the scales and all that? It was part of her, and that wasn't going to change anytime soon. She might as well embrace it, she figured.

Rinsing one more time, she stepped out of the shower and dried, then took the towel and wiped off a line on the mirror, so that she could see herself. Leaning forward before it could steam over again, she smiled, thrust out her arms, and said, "This is the new you, girl. Get used to it. This is the weapon that will see the dragon fall."

Finally, she took an offensive stance with wings thrust out, claws up at the ready, and snarled. Hot damn, she was a ferocious beast… and she loved it.

With that thought in mind, she returned to her bed, focusing to put up a mental block in case anyone else tried to enter her thoughts, and then she found herself drifting off to sleep at last.

This time, a deep slumber.

TRENT, REMALD

A second blast sounded, everyone in the whole room jerking to attention. Trent sat rigid, not wanting to break protocol by getting up to investigate, but when the third blast came, everyone was up and rushing towards the doors.

Staying close to Feras and Ezail, Trent found himself back at the area where they had landed, looking up at plumes of black smoke. Following it down, Trent could see that the smoke led to a crumbled stone building where a mass of people were shouting, motioning to others to come and help, while a group of them had already started moving rubble aside.

The two groups with Trent spent a moment looking at each other with suspicion, before charging in to help. At first as Trent rushed in, looking for anyone who might need his help, he thought the two sides were going to blame each other. But he realized this wasn't the case when the prince was the first to go dragon, taking off into the sky and heading for the hills to search for the enemy.

Regardless of all the bickering that had gone on in the castle room, the two sides were going to cooperate with each other and strike. He respected those who could take action when it was clearly called for, instead of sitting around arguing.

Meanwhile, he had spotted a man with a leg stuck under a fallen stone. Crushed, no doubt, and urgently in need of help. More stones were threatening to fall from above, so even as others shifted and took to the sky, he charged over to do what he could.

"You're going to be okay," Trent reassured him.

The injured man stared at him in bewilderment as Trent knelt, using his gold power to leverage the stone and free the man. He did the same for a woman nearby, who was also pinned down by the debris from the explosion, and then found a guy who was almost completely buried, with just his hand reaching out.

"Trent!" Feras shouted, likely for the third or fourth time, though he hadn't been paying attention.

"I have to help—"

A flash of light showed on a blade, giving Trent just enough notice to push himself back and away from his attacker. When he regained his balance and turned to strike back, he saw the woman he had helped out. She had the blade, a wicked grin spread across her face, already moving back in for another attempt to slice him open.

"Whoa, whoa," he said, hands up, trying to calm her. "I'm helping here—I'm on your side."

She snarled, lunged, and looked about to go left when instead she went right and then rebounded to strike up and under his jaw. He leaned back with it and managed to get out of harm's way, but only by losing his footing and stumbling to the ground.

Her blade came again, this time dangerously close. It would have cut into his throat if he hadn't reached up and grabbed her arm in time, and then he managed to thrust and toss her over himself. With a quick push, he was up and spinning on her, hands out.

"Again, I'm on your side," he protested, but she lunged again as Feras appeared behind her, trying to intervene.

"You're not!" Feras shouted, as someone grabbed her leg and tried to pull her back.

It hadn't hit him until then, when he noticed that the man grabbing her leg was the third one he had helped out. The guy had a gun up and aimed at her head, but she turned back and kicked it aside, while Trent took the opportunity to slam his attacker down to the ground, pinning her there.

Feras started her dragon transformation, but was caught by a blast of purple light from a device in the guy's other hand. She shook, then collapsed, causing Trent to lose any cool he might have had. He was on the man in an instant, knocking his weapon aside as the guy tried to turn it on him. A quick sweep brought the man to his back, a good stomp to the face sent blood splattering. Two more like that and the man wasn't even trying to get up.

"It's not them," Ezail called out as she appeared at her mom's side, helping her up and removing the small device that had brought her down. "Stop!"

Trent barely registered her, his foot lifting again for another stomp, when together mother and daughter pulled him away. He was about to resist, but came to himself, saw that it was them, and felt the rage within subside. Something had come over him, though he couldn't explain it.

"These ones aren't with the Exiles," Feras insisted, joining her daughter to pull Trent around a corner and out of sight of the people.

"I don't get it," he replied, trying to control his breathing. "They were attacking you."

"Some of the people have gone astray, but that doesn't mean they're with the enemy."

He blinked, shook his head.

With a sigh, Feras motioned for him to follow, and they kept moving, away from the scene of his violence. "A group in the city have started a movement against shifters. The Noshar are lumping us in with the Exiles, saying nobody should have the power we do."

Considering it, Trent had to agree. It offset the power balance to such a degree that groups like the Exiles could, unless checked, get away with almost anything. "But... couldn't they all have the power? Like... me?"

"No." She stopped under a series of porticos,

glancing around the corner to check the way. "When you entered the light, it didn't have to change you. Heal you? Yes. It heals all who enter, and is prized beyond measure for that. But very few receive its blessing."

Trent scrunched his nose at that. "I'm nobody special."

"You must have some connection to the old gods—sorry, the original Remald people, those who went to Earth, perhaps. It's possible some still remain, I suppose.

"Or maybe through contact?" Ezail offered.

"Ezail!"

The girl blushed. "I'm fifteen, mother. I know of such things."

"What things?" Trent asked.

"Must it be said?" Feras eyed him, and the uneasy way she glanced back at her daughter made it clear.

"Sorry, but... no. I've never had 'contact' with a dragon, or person from Remald."

"That you know of." She turned to Ezail. "And as for you, we need to have a talk soon."

Ezail didn't meet her eyes, but nodded.

"As for right now, we need to hurry," Feras continued. "This way."

"Where are we going?" Trent asked. "Shouldn't we be back there, helping?"

"Others will help. We're going after the attackers—those who caused the explosion."

"I don't..." He stopped talking, as it made sense. A metallic scent hit him, but it was more than that.

Opening himself to it, he could feel something pulling at him, some connection.

"If they use the same energy source, they're connected," Ezail explained, having seen the recognition in his eyes. "Likewise, if you ever need to find us, assuming we're close enough, there's a way."

"You might not have realized it," Feras added, "but in the hills when you escaped—"

"That same connection led me back." He nodded, eyes wide with the implication. "Meaning, they can also hunt us."

"If they're strong enough, and in tune with the light. Too much rage, anger, or bloodlust can block it."

"Hence, the need for meditation. And the Apophian, do they have this ability? I mean—"

"Yes, they know how to harness it. Many of them are top ranked in the matter of controlling themselves and the power of the mind. But…" Feras exchanged a nervous glance with her daughter. "Remember, that name is… best not used. Exiles, please."

"Right, the Exiles." He made a mental note of it, following as Feras led the way up a stairwell. Her focus was certainly more in tune than his own, so he trusted her to lead the hunt.

As they emerged from the porticos into a courtyard with fountains and hanging, purple flowers, Ezail muttered a curse and her mother took a deep breath. Trent didn't doubt something was wrong, but aside from sensing they were closer to their enemy, he couldn't tell what it could be.

"It's Wilnar's family house," Ezail said, explaining their reactions.

"But they aren't—"

His question was cut off by a head smashing through the wall, stones flying outward and then the head disappeared back inside, leaving a gaping hole where it had just been. A moment later, as Trent and the two ran, the head appeared again, this time catching on one of the rocks and dripping blood. Screaming came from within, but as Trent reached the front door, Wilnar came stumbling out with an arm in his hands, wires hanging from it and dripping blue liquid.

It took Trent a second to process that it couldn't be human. Feras called out to Wilnar, but he didn't seem to process this, and a moment later he was charging back in, wielding the arm as if it were a club.

Trent was the first to reach the door, following him in with his hands raised, gold light already starting to light up in preparation for an attack. Inside, a man he recognized from the hills looked up at him, leering, as three others fought with Wilnar. No room in here for Wilnar to transform, he was using the arm and a blaster, shooting and bashing, but very careful to keep his body between the attackers and a back door. Likely where his family was. It was a large house, by Earth standards. Very open, with tall glass walls and plants that hung down twice as tall as most men. One wall was completely covered with paintings and sketches, some of them clearly done by a child.

Lying on the floor along that wall was the dead body of a man, and another was over by the wall that had been bashed open. The arm that Wilnar was wielding apparently came from one of his three attackers, a woman who was clearly missing an arm. She took a couple shots from him, then the arm across the face, while the other two tried to get in to attack as well.

"Bloodbag," the man from the hills said, lifting a blade to point at Trent. "The High Drin had a feeling you'd want to come back to us."

Trent didn't respond, instead opting for helping his friend. He rolled in, making room for Feras to charge in and tackle the guy. Meanwhile, Trent was up on one knee, sending a golden blast at the closer of the three attackers going up against Wilnar.

A good shot sent the guy to the ground, but the next only exposed metal on the second attacker. Apparently, they were fighting a mix of these Exile types and androids. He'd had his experience with androids in the Marines, but for some reason hadn't expected to come across many here.

The android was on him in a second, raining down blows faster than Trent could've imagined. When Trent managed to push him away with a front kick, the android spun with a blaster nearly shooting Trent's face off. Trent felt the sting on the tip of his nose as the shot glanced off him, then his helmet formed around his face as he charged back in, blasting back at the android.

Quick enough to avoid the shots, the android ducked down, then popped up to the left. He pushed off the wall, to come at Trent with a kick. It connected and hurt like a son of a bitch, but Trent seized the opportunity. One of the other attackers had a blade drawn, pointed back as he prepared to strike. Trent lunged, and with a sweep of his foot, he had the android back and was slamming him right into the blade. All three tumbled to the ground, but Trent was up first, bringing his knee back down on the android's face.

Wilnar managed to get the next of them, but more shouts came from the other room.

"Get to them," Wilnar shouted as he smashed the life out of the two on the ground.

Trent leaped to his feet, nodded, then charged to the back room. As he ran through the doorway another explosion sounded, and the whole house rocked. Only half of the room was still standing, with two people unconscious or dead on the floor, and three more dragging off a man who resembled Wilnar.

Trent wasted no time diving after them, but his rashness cost him, as one shot flashed past him and then the next shot connected to his chest, throwing him back. He lay there gasping, then turned over and pushed himself back up. To his relief, the armor had absorbed the shot. Still, it hurt like crazy.

He had stumbled, half rolled down the debris from the explosion, and found he was now sitting outside.

Smoke rose up from the city, from other places that had been attacked, but there was no sign of the enemy.

More shots and shouts sounded from Trent's right, and he turned to gaze in that direction. Then he saw them, the ones making off with the man from Wilnar's house but they were far off, several guards in pursuit. Trent joined the chase, looking up to see a dragon in the sky closing in to help.

Wilnar came charging out from behind, shouting that they had his brother, yelling for someone to stop them. The chase led the pursued and the pursuers right up to the cliffs, and then over the edge. The hunted were gone, along with Wilnar's brother.

13

ESPINOZA, UNKNOWN PLANET C

Being back in that strange world again, Espinoza found himself first going for shelter. He had come through, not seen any sign of Ruan, and gone for the nearest hills. Trying to keep low and stay hidden hadn't been easy, considering his size and glow, but he had been searching for her for some time now and hadn't been spotted by any locals.

What worried him most was that he not only hadn't found Ruan, but that the portal he had come through was closed, and there had been no sign of Marick or the others. He had made it back last time, but wasn't clear on how the portals worked or if he would necessarily be able to find one again.

All that being the case, he was starting to think that following Ruan through had been a mistake. Better to leave her, let her take on the enemy by herself, or get killed. Then again, she was as likely to start an intergalactic incident than help anything. What did he know of her, really? Only that, while she had once been a soldier, she had then gone vampire and served that evil group of psychos.

The world was dark, which would be fine if he weren't glowing. What he could make out were tall trees, completely still in the silence that stood in stark contrast to the storm he had left behind. Hills, some bare and others in the distance covered in trees. Daring to take the high ground for a moment, at one point he crossed a stream of glowing blue water, then managed to peek over a ridge to get a view of a city in the distance. From this far away, he couldn't be sure if it was the same he'd seen before, or a different one entirely.

A strange, bullet-shaped pod flew past with a row of neon green lights underneath, a glowing white circle in the rear. Espinoza took cover, throwing himself against a tree, and staying there until it had passed, and then he got going again. Two more of these alien vehicles appeared, moving along the horizon, then were gone.

It wasn't so different from back home, he thought. That is, until he crested the next hill and spotted a massive dragon protecting what looked like a temple. He threw himself back, reached for his rifle ,only to realize he must have lost it in the chaos, and then went for the blaster. He crouched down and inched up the hill keeping out of sight, but then he froze, staring at the dragon through his sights.

No movement.

A chuckle escaped his lips as he saw the glint of moonlight off of it—bluish light, as the moon had a blue gleam to it. While it looked very much like a real-life dragon, it was a statue. And the closer he got, the more he realized it wasn't his exact idea of a dragon. Sure, it had wings. Even legs and arms with claws, but its head came together in a way that reminded him of the sandworms. Not quite the dragon-style jaw in the fantasy books he had come across years ago, but more of one that opened in three parts. If anything, it reminded him of a hybrid of a dragon and an alien... which was likely exactly what it was. Maybe inspiration years ago for both, distorted as it was passed down by word of mouth from one generation to another. Somewhat like old images of elephants and how they had some resemblance, but weren't very accurate.

The temple had a glow coming from it, so Marick approached, intrigued. More locals? A figure stepped out, looked around, and then darted out of the temple and down to the left, following what looked like a path behind it. Judging by the slight glow and way she moved, it looked like he'd found Ruan at last.

Espinoza cursed at the realization that she was putting herself out in the open way too much. He needed to get to her, so sprinted across the gap between them, a small jump and flash of flying to reach the path, and then he ran down and around to find her.

She turned, halfway through a steel door at the base of the hill. Giving him a simple nod as if she had expected him to find her there, she motioned him on to join her. She went through the door, but left it open for him.

Confusion wrinkled his brow, but he quickly followed her in, not wanting to risk any more exposure in this area.

"What are you doing?" he hissed, as the two of them entered an old storage room. The walls were made of dirt, all except along one side where they were stone.

"Looking for something," she told him, then paused, turning his way. "Where are the others?"

"Back on the other side of the portal, as far as I know. You shouldn't have come through without everyone."

"You came."

"To ensure you weren't stranded, killed."

She scoffed. "I can look after myself."

"Still... we need to find a way back."

"Of course, of course..." She went to the wall, moving along it, hands searching. "One of the Goldies, before he died... was able to pass on mental notes to this place. I think he thought it would keep him alive, or... maybe I was reading his mind."

"What sort of notes?"

She sighed, stepping back from the wall. "It wasn't clear, like he was trying to shield the thoughts from me but couldn't."

"Interesting." Espinoza had been able to get them to communicate mentally, but hadn't tried any mindreading.

Her eyes moved back over to him, then roamed

across his body. "What I find interesting is that the two of us are here. Alone."

"How so?"

"You didn't have to come for me. Maybe..." She cocked her head. "Maybe you don't feel the strong loyalty to the others that you claim."

"I'm here because of my loyalty to them."

"That so?" She stepped toward him, licked her lips, and said, "You don't have to pretend. Here, we can start over. It can be all about us—and believe me, we are powerful. This world... isn't ready for us."

At that, she stepped up, hand going to his crotch, rubbing it suggestively.

"You realize I can't feel that through this armor?" he said, and then took her hand, moving it away.

"It's the thought that counts," she said with a wink. "And the promise of what's to come."

He wasn't sure what it was about being out in space, but ever since he had arrived on this planet—scratch that, since this was a new planet—ever since he had left his galaxy, he had become the man.

She wasn't bad to look at, he had to admit. Dark, thick eyelashes that gave her an Egyptian look, tanned skin and full lips. Her nose was curved up slightly at the end in a way that reminded him of a painting he had once seen of a water nymph. His twelve-year old self had never gotten over that image, the little nymph at the edge of the water, staring at her reflection as she bathed, nude but for some well-placed leaves. Recalling that now, he couldn't deny her offer was at least tempting on the surface.

Deeper than that, though, he knew where he belonged. He was a Marine, dammit. He was loyal to his country. Had feelings for Kim and Ellins. Adding a third to the mix was selfish and stupid—the latter because he didn't begin to suppose the other two would go for it.

That, and this lady seemed to be asking him to run off, desert the others, to make some power move on this planet that Earth hadn't signed off on.

"You're crazy," he blurted out.

"Ah." She frowned, scrunched her nose, and then gestured to the exit as she turned back to the stone wall. "Don't forget to let the door hit your ass on the way out."

"That's not…" he was going to say 'how the saying goes,' but realized she was likely aware of that.

To his surprise, she found a pattern in the stones and, as she moved one down, another two over, then one up, it worked like an unlocking mechanism. A groan sounded, rock on rock, then part of it swung open to form a door. Ruan disappeared within.

Espinoza had to wonder if she had known about that all along, and wondered how much she had gotten from the Goldie. It wasn't like he had told her everything he knew of them, but he certainly planned on briefing the group. This was different. He followed her in, surprised to find a room full of carved out shelves full of supplies.

Not just any supplies, but various alien guns and ammunition, explosives, food, and more. He gaped at it, taking it in, then noticed Ruan gathering supplies, throwing them in a bag she found there that resembled a duffel.

"What are you doing?" Espinoza asked.

"Going out on my own."

"Excuse me?"

"You made it clear where you stand. No need for me to explain my actions to you."

He stepped over, grabbing her arm. "I disagree."

She glared at him, then wrenched her arm free to take more food, stuffing it in. "Earth doesn't want my kind. These people don't, either. But at least here, I can see what else there is. Look for opportunity."

"Opportunity?" Espinoza went to the entrance, glancing out.

"A new beginning."

"Shit, Ruan. We're both in this boat, okay? Marick, too."

"You think you're like me?" Ruan had abandoned her bag in an instant, jumping over the table to grab Espinoza and slam him up against the wall, knocking a box over, two cylinders rolling out. "You chose this existence. You wanted to wear the fangs because it gives you power, but not me. All I ever wanted to do was be a soldier, to serve Earth's expansion."

"Where we're headed, you still can."

She shook her head. "I did my part. They're either coming, or they aren't. Maybe by the time they get through the portal to this planet... maybe by then I'll have killed all these sons of bitches."

"That's the plan then?" He shook his head, eyeing the bag. "A lone wolf, stalking her prey."

"Picking them off one by one." She shrugged. "In large groups when possible."

"They might not be the enemy, you know. Don't do this."

"If they sent those Goldies after us... they're some of the worst enemies I've ever come across."

"Back on Earth, we've seen this scenario. Right?" Espinoza picked up what looked like an arrow to emphasize his point. "How many times have people back there gone into land that was occupied by natives, acted with violence when met with violence? Someone comes into your home with guns, you aren't going to shoot at them?"

"Of course I am."

"Exactly. But what if that person is Santa Claus, come to bring you gifts? You won't know until you take off your damn sleeping mask."

She scoffed. "Then let's take their sleeping masks off for them. Tell you what, I'll give it a chance—they don't open their eyes and look at my belly like a bowl full of jelly... they die."

With a grunt, she turned back to the bag, filled it with a couple of those cylindrical devices that had fallen, and slung the bag over her shoulder.

"Don't become a cliché," she said as she went to the

exit, glancing out to ensure none of the locals were around.

"Meaning?"

"You can talk about all that history, but we've seen the old movies. Outsider falls for the locals, helps defend them against his own? Overdone, buddy. When push comes to shove, you stick with yours."

Those words spoken, she was off. Espinoza lingered a moment longer, then packed a bag for himself as well. Not to follow in her footsteps in the slightest. His goal was only to be prepared, seeing as he had no idea where to go from there.

14

SHRINA, VIRGINIA

A hand on her shoulder woke Shrina, unknown voices coming from within the room. She bolted upright and then saw that it was the television, a screen floating on the far wall with a news anchor describing a terrible scene. Behind her, a military compound was under attack, a large man with wings flying through the sky as vampires stormed the place. Explosions, shots fired on both sides, and clearly the enemy was already in, because the soldiers were firing upon an entrance. More explosions were followed by a vampire with a fifty-cal opening up on others, then a close-up as the camera attempted to capture the winged form. The dragon perched atop the building, screams sounding as the soldiers were taken out. All they could see was his silhouette, but Shrina had no doubt it was him. She could tell he was grow-ing, too. As he became stronger, he increased in size, apparently. That could be something to worry about.

"Turn it off," Shrina said, rolling out of bed and rubbing her eyes. She became vaguely aware of the fact that she had slept in the nude, but wasn't bothered by it or the way one of the agents in the room was pointedly not looking her way. She could use her wings to cover herself, after all.

Quickly dressing and pulling on her gear, she indicated the spot where the screen had been. "Where?"

"Not far, actually," the closest agent replied. "Richards wants you and your team on the ground, ASAP."

"On it," she said, sending out the mental note for the others to get ready as well. At least two of them, she found out in rapid response, were ready. They had taken shifts throughout the night, just in case. She would have to remember to reward their good behavior.

Strolling down to the parking garage through the back stairwell—as agreed upon, to avoid drawing undue attention, she found her team waiting in the flickering yellow lights. Each of them seemed mostly healed, which was a definite plus, considering what might be in store for them that day.

"Names," she said, coming to a stop in front of them. "Trish, I know. And you are?"

"Irithu," the man next to Trish said. A tough looking man who looked to be of Indian decent, she guessed.

The others introduced themselves as Reed, Luis, and Ashu.

"Very well. And you're with me, now. My team."

Shrina walked past each of them—those who had remained. If not for having seen them as vampires, she never would have been able to tell. As it was, they looked like normal people. Well, not quite normal, as they had all been super-soldiers, before. Two of them even still wore uniforms of the New Origins corporation that had started the super-soldier program, though the logos were long gone.

They would do just fine, and along the way, maybe she could recruit more.

"Do any of you hold any hidden loyalties for the other side?" she asked, knowing they wouldn't likely say so if they did, but having to ask regardless. Having freed them by some sort of mental connection to them, she hoped she might be able to tell if they were lying.

"No," they all said at once.

"Are any of you only here because of my ability to switch you?"

The skinny one hesitated. What was his name again? She had never been the best with names, but then remembered how she had placed his name with how he looked. Reed

"I'm with you to the end," Trish said. "We never should have split ways."

"You knew her?" Irithu asked.

Trish nodded. "From before. This here is the sister of Alicia—the conqueror of New Origins."

"No shit?"

Even the one who wanted to leave them was looking at her with a new sense of awe. "Many of us were still with New Origins when it happened," he said. "Others had sided with Veles, serving under Set."

"Wait... with Veles *and* Set?" She shook her head, trying to clear her mind and recall whether she had heard of those two being connected in any way in the past. No, not that she could recall.

"Up on the station, yes. Set served directly under Veles in the rebellion against New Origins. Together—"

"And since?" she interrupted. "What about now? I mean, did Set serve Veles up to the end?"

Trish frowned. "Was there an end for him?"

"Yes. I killed him."

The others shared a look, as that was apparently news to them.

"Good," Trish spat. "And... yes, as far as I know, Set was still working with Veles. To be fair, we never saw them together, but had no reason to believe otherwise."

"There were calls," Irithu said. "From D.C. And I heard him say Veles once or twice."

Shrina considered this, finding it deeply troubling. "Keep it to yourselves, for now. At least until I figure out what to do with the information."

"You got it," Trish said. The others nodded.

Anticipation bubbled up through the team as they made their way, Shrina trying not to think about Veles and any sort of other role he might have played in the grand scheme of things. If he was at all responsible for the rising of the dragon, he would answer for his crime. But for now, they had a fight to get to.

"Can you go any faster?" she asked Irithu, who was

driving one of the SUV-style pods they had taken. Shrina rode with him and Trish, and the other three were in a second pod.

He didn't respond, but moved his hands over the control screen and overrode some of the systems commands. The pod lurched forward, almost stalled, then picked up the pace.

"That's more like it," Trish said with a laugh, pounding the ceiling. At a look from Shrina, she shrugged, "What, because I'm a vampire and we're riding off to certain death, I'm supposed to not have fun?"

"I'm still figuring that part out," Shrina admitted. How much of her old life was she allowed to have, what with this new responsibility looming over her?

"Well, you do." Trish leaned forward, hand on Irithu's shoulder. "We're going to make the most out of this, aren't we, big guy?"

"I don't follow," he replied, not turning away from the display and the path they were taking.

"Yeah, you do." She winked at Shrina, leaning back and then closing her eyes.

Irithu glanced back, finally. Judging by the curiosity in his look and the way his eyes roamed over Trish, he knew very well what she had in mind. It took Shrina a second to catch on, but then she allowed a smile. Maybe Trish had the right idea. They weren't necessarily going to live long at the rate they were throwing themselves into the path of danger, so why not live life to its fullest in the meantime? For Trish that might mean screwing this guy's brains out, but for Shrina, she wasn't sure. It wasn't that, at least she knew.

Traveling the world had always been something she enjoyed, but with her sister gone, that didn't exactly matter anymore. Everything else that came up had the same hollowness to it, so that Shrina came to one conclusion—get Alicia, then have fun. Put everything into killing the dragon, so that she could enjoy the moments. In the meantime, she wasn't going to stand in the way of the others if they wanted to have a good time.

In a sense, they were putting their lives on the line for her.

"Let me drive," she said. "You two... do your thing."

"We're not going to do anything with you right here with us," Irithu replied, shaking his head. But when he noticed Trish with one eye open and on him, he scooted out of the way, making room for Shrina to work her way forward. It wasn't easy, what with the wings, but she made it.

"I've got a solution," Shrina said. When he was gone, she pulled up the holoscreen controls and found what she was looking for. With a wink at Trish, she made a divider go up. A giggle came from Trish, and then a gasp from Irithu before the sound and sight were cut off.

In a way, the solitude of being in the front without having to see or hear them was refreshing. Not that she was completely alone, as she still had her mental connection with the vampires on her team, a fact that became slightly weird when the pod started rocking. She even found her body tingling with pleasure, and had to figure out a way to sever the connection. It worked, but she sat up, listening and wondering if that would mean they would revert back to being under the dragon's control.

A second later, the pod rocked again and there was a long moan, so she covered her ears and tried her best not to laugh. They were fine, she realized, and focused back on looking at their destination, wondering about the fight to come.

When she was just about to lower the divider to check on them, the pod started rocking again, and she had to roll her eyes. How much energy did they have?

"Don't exhaust yourselves back there," she called out, unsure whether they could even hear her.

"Shut up or you'll ruin the moment!" Trish called out.

Shrina pretended to zip her lips, then leaned out and watched a city disappear below. Several store fronts, a line of billboards that glowed with neon lights, and pods zipping around. Then it was gone, replaced with trees.

"Dammit," the voice of Reed came through the line from the other pod. "You seeing this?"

Shrina frowned, turning to the display on the pod and instantly feeling her gut clench up. An image of vampires running off, some driving newly acquired military equipment. A fighter jet falling from the sky, exploding.

"They're on the move," Shrina said, checking the timing. "We're not going to make it in time."

"I'll try to analyze the direction of movement," Luis said. "See if we can redirect and cut them off, but... damn."

"What?"

"They're moving in at least three different directions, and already going dark."

She cursed, hit the dash, and then stewed on it for a moment. They were so close, but it wasn't going to be enough. At least fifteen minutes out still, she couldn't even see the fighting that the videos were capturing. Even that was mostly dying out as the vampires seemed to have gotten what they'd come for.

"Everything... okay?" Trish asked, divider coming down. She leaned forward, not bothering to cover up.

Shrina regretted the view of the two wrapped around each other's nude bodies, pushing Trish's head back as she said, "Finish up, get dressed. We're almost there... but don't expect a fight."

"Damni—" Trish started, cut off by Shrina putting the divider up again. She was happy for the girl to be getting hers, but now had both the letdown of not making it in time plus the image of Irithu in her mind. Not that he was something she wanted, but a reminder that she not only didn't have anyone like that, and maybe never would again, wasn't exactly the right medicine for her mood at the moment.

When they lowered the pods to the ground and the

teams exited, it was clear they were too late. Military drones were already scanning the area, some Marine Corps MPs approaching Shrina and her team at first, but getting a message—likely from Richards—halfway there and stopping. One of them gave them a nod, then turned back to his duties. Medic bots were already tending to the wounded, and there wasn't much to be done there.

At least Trish and Irithu were radiant, glowing with excitement in spite of the letdown at not getting a good fight. Reed and Luis noticed, and were giving them a hard time about it, asking what had happened on the ride over, but Shrina stepped away from them, eyes scanning their surroundings.

The dragon was long gone, but something else was happening to Shrina now that she stood there, looking out at the trees and wispy clouds. A sense, like the pulling she had felt before. She was connected with him, or he was calling her. If it was the latter, she might very well walk into a trap, but didn't give a damn. She had to go.

A glance back at her team showed they were ready, Trish standing tall, hands balled into fists, Irithu crouched, eyes searching. Reed and Luis were awaiting orders. One was missing.

"Where's Ashu?" Shrina asked.

Instead of answering, Irithu pointed.

"Nobody thought it worth mentioning that she ran off?" Shrina asked.

"At first," Trish answered. "But you looked deep in

thought, and we figured following her might make more sense."

Actually, it did. Especially since Ashu was not going in the same direction as she felt the pull toward the dragon. She was likely heading for a recruiting office, hearing the sort of siren's call that had pulled at Shrina overseas. She could go there, first. A minor detour that could possibly help in the long run.

Gathering the rest of her team, they returned to their SUV-pods. As much as she wanted to simply take off in pursuit, flying on her own, it was still best to not put herself out there for the world to see.

"Next move?" Reed asked, leaning out from the open door of the other pod.

"Follow me," Shrina said, taking the driver seat of her pod. "We're going to do some recruiting."

15

TRENT, REMALD

Trent was the first to reach the drop-off, staring in confusion. Where had they gone? Dragons soared overhead, others swooping down. From what he could see, though, they weren't finding the aggressors, either.

Simply no sight of them. Gone.

Feras flew up in front of him, flapping her massive wings, and turned, waiting. Getting the hint, Trent ran and jumped onto her back. He felt like he would slip, but she flew down and then up, giving him the chance to get the hold he needed.

"Where could they have gone?" he shouted, figuring she wouldn't have brought him like this unless she had some sort of an idea.

I'm hoping you can help in that regard, she replied, flying past her daughter as the younger dragon circled around, clearly frustrated.

Trent strained his eyes, calling up his gold vision to

help. He focused on his breathing, the meditation techniques he had learned in his younger years, hoping that could help him with the hunt. They flew down the cliff face, seeing no way in, then to the waters below, where Trent strained his eyes to see into the water itself, thinking maybe the enemy had gone for a dive, perhaps.

Nearby, the prince flew, too, roaring with frustration. He nearly reached the cliffs, then flapped hard to stop himself and shot up almost vertically.

As water swirled with the current caused by the downward draft from the prince's wings, Trent noticed something. He guided Feras closer, but didn't see it again.

What?

"A dark opening, maybe. A cave."

She flew by again, and while he didn't see anything, this time he caught the scent. Without a doubt, this was the convincing he needed.

"I'm going in," he said, and stood up on her back.

You're crazy, she replied, but flew him back toward the spot.

"Whatever's necessary." Close to the point, he jumped, diving headfirst. As the water came up to engulf him, he had a horrible vision of sinking to his death. To his relief, however, the armor burst into light and formed like robes around him, then went tight and soft, like a wetsuit. Cold water hit, but he was mostly insulated. Then he was pushing through toward the clear opening ahead. Sunlight shone through in lines, large fish that reminded him of legless cows moved out of his way, and he was soon entering the dark cave.

As he had expected, it went back into a cavern. His gold outfit provided light, and soon he was moving through the tunnel to a point where it went up and he was crawling onto dry stone. Light flashed bright and fast, and he threw himself back just as an explosion went off, sending fire through the passage and rocks crumbling down.

One pegged him, trapping his leg as more threatened to fall down on him.

Trent gasped for air, pulling at the rock on his leg. He didn't want to have to use his powers, knowing that doing so pulled from a reserve that wasn't limitless. He was just starting to make some headway with the first rock, when more began to fall. Heart thudding, he turned and clawed his way out of harm's reach. Stones fell, but he was now sheltering under a ledge, and able to move back toward the direction he wanted to go.

This time, as he progressed, he stayed alert for whatever it was that had gone off. Some form of fancy Claymore? At one point, he knelt in the shadows, eyeing a shape he could see in the gloom ahead. It took him a few seconds to realize it was just a stone. He moved faster, continuing with caution, until the metallic scent was unmistakable. Some of those bastards were definitely down in these caverns, he wasn't about to sit around and wait for the others to catch up. He charged forward until he reached the corner, where he saw them turn toward him. With a silent curse, he made his glow fade. Charging through darkness lit up like a Christmas tree with gold light wasn't the smartest tactic.

"Is that you, Earther?" one of them said.

"Bright as the sun, charging at us like he owns the world." The second one laughed. "That's him all right."

"Come on out so we can taste your blood. "

"Where did you take him?" Trent ducked around the corner, already starting to charge before they could respond.

A blast went off, lighting up the tunnel, but this time the explosion came nowhere near to hitting Trent. With his glow switched off, there was no way he could be seen down here. But Trent had counted on them firing, the blast from the gun telling him exactly where they were. He landed on the first, with an elbow to the nose, and had the man down. Another blast went off, and the shout came from another.

"Where?"

"You stupid—" the second started, but Trent had managed to get the blaster and shoot.

"This is your last chance. Where?" Trent took the blaster and pressed it up against the person, but he was having none of it.

"Go back home, outsider," He hissed.

Instead of firing, Trent called upon his powers again. He pushed his fingers against the man's forehead, thumb on his temple. His skull lit up, smoke rising from the man's temple as Trent's fingers burned into it.

"I already gave you your warning…" Trent growled, unsure of how far to go with this, and said, "Consider this your only second chance in life, that you'll never get again."

The man growled, then started to scream but he still wasn't willing to give anything up. Trent hated it, but he only had one choice. He let him go, then dealt the final blow and ended the man.

Trent charged further into the tunnels, his vision going red, his feet stumbling. Suddenly his world tilted left, then right, and he held out a hand to catch himself on the wall. He tried to regain his footing but overcompensated in the opposite direction so that he ended up on the rocky ground, lying on his side.

Trent pushed himself up to his hands and knees, shook his head to try to clear his mind, and looked up. The walls were still moving, left and right, right and left. Whatever was happening, he knew it wasn't real, but was all in his head. This idea was reinforced when a rage built up in him that he'd felt before. A bloodlust that he couldn't explain.

"Ohklon, where are you?"

No answer came, but the scent grew stronger. Along with it, came images of dragons, flying in circles around him as the rocks and earth crumbled away. Then he was a dragon, black and purple spreading out from him, taking over everything that he was. Two other dragons flew his way, attacking him with flames. He struck back on instinct, everything about him as a dragon taking over, taking control. Then he had one of the dragons, teeth at its neck, pulling ripping.

The dragon fell, and as it did so the magic of the dragon faded, revealing Ezail, throat torn open. Horrified at what he'd just done, Trent threw himself down at her side, searching for any way to help her, as her last breath of life gurgled out through the blood. Feras appeared at his side, and stared down in horror.

"What have you done?" she cried.

He shook his head, backing away from the body. He wasn't a dragon at all, only a man.

"You see what you are?" Ohklon said. "It's in your very nature, it's who you are. You can never allow them to live on as they are."

"You're wrong."

"We shall see."

Abandoning the gold light, Trent focused entirely inward, on his mind, and there he found the self-control to be able to repel any outside force exerted by Ohklon. This time, when he looked up the world wasn't spinning or shifting. The red from his vision was gone. No sign of Feras or Ezail, and he was up and running again. More tunnels led to yet more tunnels. It was there that he came across one of those explosive devices, but was able to avoid it by using a different path. There were multiple levels here, sometimes they would take him up, others down. He felt like he'd been running for far too long now, and for too long he'd found no more sign of those he pursued. This was without a doubt the way the enemy had come. But there were too many options, the scent too distant now to give him anything to go on.

He had failed.

Making his way back up, he thought about how he would tell Wilnar. But instead, found himself more determined than ever. He felt stronger now, and he vowed he would find others to return with him, to flush out the enemy, to find his friend's brother.

16

ESPINOZA, UNKNOWN PLANET C

Now that he had found Ruan, and lost her, he at least had a reason to look for a way back. She was on her own at this point, maybe they'd be able to reconnect with her to find her and convince her this wasn't the way. Maybe Marick would, anyway. And for that, Espinoza found himself getting fairly pissed off that Marick hadn't been the one to come through in the first place. After all he had been the one closest to Ruan. She was pretty much a newcomer to the rest of them.

Taking the new equipment, Espinoza slung his bag on his back and started off for the hills again. By this point, the glow was gone and so he felt more secure moving in the darkness. He had strapped on what he could. A couple of blasters, some items that look like grenades, incendiary devices in his side holsters, but the rest of it went into the bag. If he was lucky he wouldn't need it.

Running along the grassy hill, he remembered images of the first recon missions through the gateway to the stars. Hadn't it looked much more like this? Now that he was focused on it, he even noticed how some of the rocks in the distance rose up in a sort of curved shape. It resembled a witch's hat, and back home that's exactly what they called it. Find the witch's hat they had said, and there it was. Could the machines they'd sent through meant for them to come to this planet all along?

The implications of that thought were making his head spin, so he forced himself to focus on the here and now, focused on reconnecting with Marick and the others, and hoping that Ruan wouldn't cause too much trouble in the meantime. He had his head down, scanning the area for anything living. So far he'd only spotted a couple of small flying creatures that he imagined were like birds by the strange sounds they were making. Something similar to a crow's caw, but with a little bit of a screech to it. His suit registered that the temperature was in the low sixties, and considering how pleasant it all seemed, so much so that he seriously considered taking off his suit and relaxing for a while. But that was no good. Everything could fall apart if the team wasn't reunited ASAP.

When he had a view of the city, he knelt down and squinted, searching the outline of first the walls, and then the objects close to the walls. But it wasn't there that he found the gateway he was looking for. Instead, he found those curved metal, leaf-like structures on the inner curve of another hill. He strained his eyes to see past that and indeed there was another one on the next hill. He wondered if it made sense then, that there would be one on his hill. Darting forward among the trees, he came to a spot where the decline was steep, and he could look down and see the tip of one of those metallic gates.

It wasn't open yet, but there were also no signs of people nearby that he could see from this angle. Working his way around to make sure, he slowly descended, having to climb down a steep rocky portion of the hill at one point, and then made it to the other side of a clearing.

Sounds of a scuffle came from ahead, and he thought for sure it would be Ruan. Charging forward he came face-to-face with two young looking male locals, both with a slight silver glow to their hair. No sign of Ruan anywhere.

Both turned to him with looks of bewilderment on their faces, which morphed to shock on one and horror on the other. The terrified one fell to his knees as he made a wailing sound, while the second one stepped forward, hand up as if to touch Espinoza and see if he was real.

"Open the portal," Espinoza commanded, making his voice sound as deep and authoritative as he could.

"You speak... our language?" the boy said.

Now that he mentioned it, Espinoza wasn't sure

that was the case. A similar feeling had come over him when the boy spoke, and he was fairly certain the gold power had intercepted his vocal commands, adjusting what he said to fit the boy's comprehension, and vice versa. If that was the case, he wondered about those like Ellins who couldn't use the gold, or what would happen when it wore off completely within him.

"Open the portal," he said again, indicating the gate. "Now."

The two looked at him, then one—the terrified one—lunged with a knife that he had apparently drawn. Espinoza simply stepped back while swinging his forearm in and connecting with the boy's forearm, hitting the knife out of his hand, so that the blade went clattering across the stones next to the gate.

A look of surprise took the other boy, who grabbed the attacker and said, "Are you mad? You shouldn't have done that!"

"He's right, you shouldn't have." Espinoza took a step toward them, but they broke off. At the same moment, a shout came from the right, followed by the sound of shots fired. Forgetting these two, Espinoza darted up the ridge to a point where he could see.

There, moving among the trees, was the floating, gold form of Marick. And on the ground, Ellins! They had made it. He gave up on this portal and ran to meet them. Unfortunately, without the level of gold power he'd had, now he couldn't simply fly, though he tried at first. A good jump and he went stumbling, having to catch himself.

A second later, he was running again, this time much more reliant on his own abilities. The suit's thrusters were no good at this point, but he was still feeling energized, plus he had rested while dealing with the whole Ruan situation. Physically, anyway—her whole abandoning of them had caused him a bit of mental strain.

Reaching the next hill and starting to make his way up, he heard more shouting, followed by Ellins calling somebody a coward, followed by a slew of curses. He pushed himself harder, leaping over stones and grabbing trees to pull himself up, then came upon a ledge where he could look up and see the portal between the gate, Marick there darting about, fighting off a group of locals firing at them from the bushes down the hill. Ellins was attempting the same, but closer to the gate and holding her position.

It hit him then that the rest of the group wasn't through yet.

"Marick!" Espinoza shouted, then changed his trajectory to join the fight. He hoped to draw the attention away, so that Marick could get back to the gate and pull in the rest of the team. "Go!"

Reaching the point where the fighting was going on, Espinoza was faced with a conundrum. These weren't the Goldies, but they were still trying to shoot at his companions. They were defending their homes, but unlike the Goldies, didn't seem to be a major threat. They shot, but stuck to their cover, and even the weapons they were using didn't strike him as impressive. At most, they would ding off the Marine's body armor.

With that in mind, he went for the stun option. Target one was no problem—an older man who turned with a half-yelp before the hit came and sent him onto his back, out cold. A woman had heard the sound though, and appeared a second later charging out from the bushes firing shots. Two more dinged off of his armor, the rest hitting the trees behind him or the hill opposite. She tried to then take him by slamming her shoulder into him, but that only sent her to the ground with a grunt.

"Stay down," Espinoza commanded. "I'm not here to—"

Another shot from nearby sounded loud, grazing his nose. It was enough to startle him, so that when the woman below acted at the same time, he lashed out, slamming the stunner of his fist into her chest. She convulsed, lying there and holding her gut, while he charged the young man who was about to fire again. The slight wound was already healing, but it stung like hell. A block up sent the next shot wide, a good punch to the head crumpled the guy. Espinoza didn't envy the headaches these guys would have when they woke up, but it was better than the alternative—death.

Marick appeared above and shouted, "I'm going back for more."

"What've you been doing this whole time?" Espinoza growled back, already working his way up and ignoring a couple of shots from behind.

No answer came, as Marick had already turned and likely gone through. A short climb later, Espinoza had found Ellins and gave her a nod.

"Stun shots?" he asked.

"Doing my best."

He couldn't help himself, leaning in and grabbing her close and then pressing his lips to hers. When she pulled him back with more force, passionately kissing him, he nearly forgot they were on an alien planet and being shot at.

"Get a room," Kim said, and they pulled apart to see her coming running up from the gate, Marick darting back through. "And while you're at it... send me an invite."

Espinoza chuckled nervously, but watched as Ellins moved to help her up, then stood back so Kim could kiss him, too. He held the latter, still overwhelmed by this situation, and looked down at a man who was staring at the three of them wide-eyed. The man smiled, seeming like he was going to give him a thumbs up, but instead lifted a pistol to shoot.

"Faceplates on," Espinoza commanded as he sent a stunner shot at the man, at the same time stepping into the line of fire. He could heal, but the two women couldn't. Their armor was likely to protect them, but images of their faces being blown off while kissing him made his stomach churn.

Another of theirs down, Espinoza noted three pods coming their way.

"Saw them," Ellins said, moving back behind cover.

"Hurry your ass," Kim said, faceplate down now and looking down at the gate. She moved back, too, while Espinoza sent a couple of warning shots into the trees below, where he saw movement.

"We need to keep them off of us," Espinoza said, weighing his options. "How are they keeping the gate open?"

"There." Ellins indicated the gate, where several slightly glowing gold stones were inserted at points along the metal. "Some sort of fuel, likely related to the energy sources that fuels the Goldies."

"And you all, back there," Kim added.

"Right." He noted the glow was still there at least, so the gate probably had some time, still. Now the push from below made sense—they were trying to deactivate the gate, upon realizing outsiders were coming through. Another glance up at the pods, closing fast.

Ellins cleared her throat, and he noted her hands on her hips, staring at him.

"What?" he asked.

"To be clear, I still outrank you. I call the shots."

"Of course." He said that, but his thoughts were more along the lines of, *What? Really? After that kiss, and considering my new abilities?* None of that needed to be said, though, because she was technically right. At some point, they hoped to connect with Earth forces, and he needed to remember where he stood in the system.

"You and I try to draw them away," Ellins said, indicating the pods. "Kim, make sure those people don't shut down the portal."

"Terms of Engagement?"

"Try to avoid it, but lethal force if necessary. Our priority right now is having the team together."

"Roger that."

Kim's voice had been a bit cold. Maybe she was having issues with chain of command now, too, having shared a bed with both of them. The whole rule against fraternization was starting to make more sense. Then again, maybe she was more annoyed that Espinoza and Ellins were running off together without her. As the corporal, she didn't have a say in the matter.

Either way, they knew their roles, and so Ellins motioned to move out. Espinoza followed with a nod to Kim, meaning it more as a sort of good-bye kiss type nod, but he worried as he went that it had come off as more formal. Dammit, Marines weren't supposed to be worried about offending each other on an emotional level when in combat.

He cursed himself for letting the situation get to this point, but also he knew in his heart that he wouldn't change a thing. It was stressful up there, in their predicament. Having people to lean on and care for helped him through it—Kim and Ellins were perfect in that regard.

One of the pods swerved the moment Espinoza and Ellins appeared on an open area of the hill, shooting down on them. They dove for cover and returned fire. It wasn't until a shot from Ellins caused the first pod to

swerve as it got hit—having a hard time recovering—
that a second pod came their way. Likely it was
responding to a distress call. The third, however,
continued its trajectory toward the gate.

A shot came from that direction, a loud crack
sounding as it connected, but the pod continued on.

"Good shot, Kim," Espinoza muttered as he checked
his gear, opting for a grenade. "Cover me."

"Don't do anything stupid," Ellins replied.

"Too late."

He was up and running, blaster sending off shots
from his left hand, right with the grenade at the ready.
When the two pods were close, a whirring sound as
they prepared to fire on him, he jumped as high as his
modified muscles and enhanced suit would let him. It
was damn high. Enough so that he found himself
wondering if gravity here worked differently than back
home. It hadn't seemed to on the sandworm planet, but
this was a different place entirely, and he had no reason
to assume it would be the same.

Shots rang out, exploding the hillside where he had
just been but too slow to follow his movement. At the
arc of his jump, he lobbed the grenade and grinned,
gripping his blaster with both hands as he started
his fall.

"Watch this," he muttered through comms.

"Got my popcorn ready," came a reply from Franco.
He'd made it through!

No time to celebrate though, because Espinoza was
in the middle of falling, squeezing out blasts. He had no

idea how long that grenade would take to go off, it being a local one and all, so he intended to take control of the situation. One good hit and a ball of flames shot out, rocking both pods so that they lost control. The already damaged pod spun wildly, slamming into a tree and then hitting the ground with a thud. Shots continued to pepper the ground from the other as it reeled up, the driver clearly trying to compensate and avoid crashing by flying straight up. Intent didn't go far though, not with the pod in the condition it was from the blast, and the attempt spiraled the ship back and toward the gate.

"Shit!" Franco shouted, and a second later there was a loud crashing sound.

Espinoza landed with a thud, the impact rocking him, and then spun while asking what happened.

"Crash, dipshit," Franco replied. "I'm okay, but lost sight of Marick."

"Get on him," Ellins interjected. "Espinoza, we need to get over there and—"

A new barrage of shots cut her off, and overhead a ship lowered through the clouds, uncloaking as it did so. Apparently, this wasn't exactly some backwater planet. Instead of the barrage of missiles Espinoza expected, several gold forms appeared, diving from the ship.

Shouts and cheers rose up from the hill, and trees rustled as the locals seemed to be retreating.

"Ellins?" Espinoza asked.

"I'm good. Dove for cover."

"You seeing this?"

"Seeing… oh, damn."

"I count ten of them, at least," Kim cut in. "I'm here with Marick, and Franco, we have eyes on you."

"You three stick together," Ellins said. "We'll work toward each other."

"Roger that." Kim cursed again, then shouted, "Watch out!"

Another barrage of shots came from the ship, followed by an explosion that hit the hill between the two groups. Espinoza was close enough to feel the blast and be hit by the barrage of dirt and tree trunks that flew at him, smoke filling the sky as two Goldies landed on either side of him. Only, here they were different from before. Not Goldies, he realized when they got close, firing on him. First of all, they had eyes underneath their faceplates. Helmets almost like the Marines, but with visors that went up at the sides resembling wings. Sure, they wore gold robes, but they wore armor that glowed gold and seemed to be embedded with small stones like the ones he had seen at the gate.

It started to make sense, then. Like the stone before that had started to drain his power, or absorb it, these stones could be charged and used to enhance the armor, open the gate, and provide energy in what he guessed were numerous other ways.

Holy hell, he was looking forward to learning more about those stones. For now though, he was ducking behind cover, returning fire, and trying to get a grasp on the situation.

Espinoza took a step back, then noticed Ellins halfway down the hill with three Goldies moving in on her. Hating to abandon his position, he retreated to her side, the two standing back to back, weapons drawn and shooting.

More shots were going off up the hill, explosions too, and Kim was shouting, "They're pressing us hard, trying to split the group!"

"Stay close!" Marick could be heard in the background, through her comms, then said something else that was drowned out by another explosion. All that came through was, "Don't let them—"

The enemy forces were moving in, blasts of gold coming from their weapons and making Espinoza truly hate the color. If he ever saw gold jewelry again, he swore at that moment he would punch the wearer in the face.

More ships lowered from the sky. Targeting the hill and the portal.

"We're going around the backside of the hill," Franco said, voice cutting through the comms. "Meet at..." His voice cut out, heavy interference like screeching cutting through.

"Comms off!" Ellins shouted, voice coming through her faceplate instead of comms. "They're throwing interference."

"The others are pulling back," Espinoza replied,

firing at one of the attackers, trying to get a sense of where to meet with Kim, Franco, and Marick.

"Stay with me," Ellins commanded, and turned to lead him down the hill. As shots sizzled through the air behind them, Ellins and Espinoza sprinted down and away from their entry point and teammates.

17

SHRINA, VIRGINIA

D riving pods at full throttle was exhilarating, especially when you knew they could self-drive. For one, it was like refusing to let some machine dictate how fast she could go. Shrina was overthrowing her oppressive pod wanna-be master, going all out to find the local vampire recruitment station.

While not exactly a 'station,' it was exactly as she had expected. Another spot, kind of underground and in the form of an old half-buried military bunker. She left the pod and others behind, not bothering to see if they were keeping pace as she charged in. It was a simple matter of catching this group of vampires off guard, and then pulling at their wills just as she had with the others.

The first batch were instantly changed, red in their eyes fading out as they turned to her in confusion and curiosity. Some were able to resist, but all she had to do was shout for the others to restrain them and then she had her army. Only two had to be taken out completely, and her new soldiers disposed of the bodies.

She grinned, looking out over the twenty or so new recruits to her side. Sometimes, life didn't have to be complicated. You want something, you go out and get it. Next though, would be the dragon himself. She refused to believe that would come so easy.

"Indoctrinate them," she told Trish.

"You got it, boss." Trish stepped forward, calling them together, quickly going over the new deal. They were free now, but the dragon had the influence to control them, an influence Shrina seemed to have as well, but she wouldn't use it on them. They could make their own choice about whether to stay and fight, or go into hiding.

All stayed.

Turning her attention to the dragon, Shrina pushed out a message. *Come and get me.* Then she went to find a restroom. Unfortunately, being a demi-dragon didn't get rid of that need. When she was done and stepped out, drying her hands, Trish walked over, glancing around at her new army, standing by for orders.

"What are we doing?" Trish asked.

Shrina grinned. "Waiting."

With a nod, Trish turned back to the new recruits and started barking out orders. Shrina had nearly forgotten that the woman had been a soldier with New Origins, and was used to this stuff. More so than herself, really. It helped to have a general with combat knowledge at her side.

She paced, watching them move into defensive positions, some taking up patrols, others going for rest. One group was sent for food while others started training, the latter ensuring each vampire they brought into their fold was on the same basic level of fighting skills. They didn't have much time, but since a good portion of them had been former New Origins soldiers like Trish and Pete, it wasn't very difficult.

"The dragon isn't here," Trish pointed out as the two watched the other vampires as they stood at their lookouts. Some had geared up, taken various positions of defense, while others went below as reserves.

"He's coming." Shrina froze in place, sensing something else. Her head jerked left, eyes focusing to see shapes approaching. Pods. FBI pods. Dammit, she had hoped to not have to drag Richards and the rest into this.

The pods pulled up outside, Richards and Chung the first to exit.

"What were you thinking?" Richards asked as they stormed over. "You think we don't have trackers in the pods? You can't just take off and..." He glanced around at the army of vampires, anger turning to confusion. "What exactly are you doing?"

"Forming an army," she replied. "I've taken more, or freed them, you could say. Now... we're waiting for him to come to us."

"And he's coming," Trish assured them.

Shrina smiled, nodding.

"Well, damn. You're sure?" He motioned back to the other pods, then spoke into comms as he said, "Weaponize. The shit's about to hit the fan."

"You can send them home." Shrina's eyes roamed the horizon as her internals searched for signs of how far out the dragon was. Not far. "No sense having families lose their loved ones today."

"Everyone here has family, of some sort," he countered.

"Vampires?" Trish spoke up. "To them, we're as good as dead."

"You're really not." He nodded at Shrina. "She's family, to me. Of a sort—and I haven't lost one bit of respect or love for the woman."

"Watch it now," Shrina said, teasingly.

"Not in any inappropriate way. As a sister in arms. As part of the family. Every one of you here still has a life worth fighting for, and people who care."

"Maybe not all of us," Irithu growled.

He shrugged. "Some of my people can say the same. Point is, we all know what we're getting into here. The fight against this thing, this 'dragon,' as you call him, it's bigger than all of us."

"Yeah, it means a lot," Shrina agreed.

"That, and actually bigger." He swiped a hand over his wrist device, pulling camera footage. "This was taken outside of Norfolk no more than an hour ago."

On the screen, the dragon was at least twice as large as when they had last seen an image of him. He was growing at an alarming rate, apparently feasting on soldiers as he and his followers took out the Marines. As drones moved in to shoot at him and his followers, the dragon transformed fully into an actual dragon, roaring and then letting out a breath—not of fire, but a burst of lightning strikes that shot out and chained between the drones, frying them all at once.

"Damn," Shrina said, gulping. "I was about to say that if you're here, we might as well call in the big guns."

"Governments are rallying, sending fighter planes and more, but everything they've sent so far, he's been able to take down. He has weapons, too, including missile lock, AA, and EMPs. It's not looking good—but more than that, they're easily able to go dark, get out of sight. At his size, it's impressive."

"Because he can shape shift," Shrina noted, watching as he returned to his humanoid shape, albeit still twice as large as most men.

"Exactly."

They watched a moment longer, then Richards swiped the screen away.

"Any news on… up there?" Shrina asked, nodding to the sky and beyond.

"Actually, yes." He paused, pulling up another screen. This one showed communication logs, including a message that was sent by Corporal Kim, one of those who had survived. "It seems they've come into contact with the locals, and it doesn't look like relations are going to be all high fives and hugs just yet." Closing it, he added, "Washington belongs to one of the countries under Global Command considering going back through the gateway. Our troops need backup, and maybe a ride home."

"Maybe?"

He nodded. "Top brass still hasn't decided what sort of threat the locals are. Whether we can ultimately befriend them or…"

"Take them out." She shook her head at the thought. "We can't go into somebody else's home and simply exterminate them."

"Wouldn't be the first time. But I'm on your side—it wouldn't be right."

She grunted, looking out over the land, and felt the pulse of danger. The dragon. A moment later, she saw something coming in fast.

"No way…" Taking a step closer, she squinted to better see. Sure enough, it looked like the enemy had acquired a torpedo-class transport ship—basically for rapid troop movement, and armed for sieges.

"I'm calling this in," Richards said. "Getting the military ready to do whatever they can… in case we fail."

"Smart," Shrina replied, but her focus wasn't on him.

She was one-hundred percent focused on the incoming transport ship, as she crouched down ready for action. As soon as the vampires begin parachuting out, some simply going for the ground running without even the benefit of chutes, she charged, shouting for her own side to move as well. She leapt up and then swooped down on the incoming enemy, shooting as she went. She was amongst them. She would strike, leap up and rain down bullets, and then throw herself down to shoot some more before resorting to hand-to-hand when they got too close.

She kept glancing around, looking for signs of Alicia, or others she might know. But none came. Not even a sign of the dragon himself.

"Shrina!" Trish called out.

Turning to see a flurry of dirt and leaves being whipped up by beating wings, Shrina froze at what she now saw. The dragon was there, behind them. He had used the transport as a distraction. Shrina slammed into two of her opponents, throwing knees and elbows, blasting her way through the melee, before she was able to make it to the air and flap back toward the dragon. She was nearly there when a shout came out and Irithu collapsed.

The dragon took a step toward Trish as well, but that was when Shrina landed with her attack. A flying kick to the back of the beast sent him sprawling forward. He would've toppled over Trish if not for the fact that she managed to scramble out of the way. Trish sent a blast back his way as she ran to help Irithu, and Shrina took the advantage.

The fight between Shrina and the dragon felt just like those times when, as a child, Shrina had challenged her dad to a sparring match. Only, her dad's standard back then was nothing compared to this contest. The dragon slammed her again and again in the chest. On the third blow, she felt the air being knocked completely out of her lungs and she was fighting to catch her breath, regain herself and move back in for the fight. She tried flying but he simply grabbed her by the ankle and slammed her to the ground. Bile and blood in her mouth, Shrina kicked free and rolled. Not fast enough, though, because he landed a stop kick to her thigh.

"You can quit now," the dragon said. "But that isn't like you, is it?"

"Never." She attempted to stand, the pain in her thigh too much to keep her steady.

"Good. Pretend this doesn't hurt, and know that I'm doing it for you." He stepped in and brought his large meaty fist into her face.

She fell back again, wings catching her, but everything went black for a moment, then faded back in with red. Another fist. Shrina fell to the ground, stunned that this was happening.

"My name is Kengris," the dragon said, taking large strides as he approached. "King over all. Master of this world now, and destined to be master once again of many more to come, once we are together again."

Together? Shrina frowned and tried to back away, but hit the wall of a building. Nowhere to go, she tried to stand. In a flash, Kengris was there, wings spread out behind him and hands slamming her into the wall, teeth bared in a snarl. Except, then he looked remorseful, starting to pull her in, even wrap his arms around her.

"I'm sorry, child," he said.

Before she could respond, shots pinged off his scaly body, one hitting a patch of flesh on his neck. He growled and cast her aside, turning on the shooter. In two steps he was in the air, transforming to a full dragon to attack the shooters. Shrina pulled herself up and turned, able to now see pods with Marines, rifles aimed in on him, unleashing again. Drones flew about up there, barraging him with bullets, and more were incoming.

Holy hell, there were a lot of those drones and pods, and more troops and their mechs approaching on the ground. Whatever this Kengris guy had in mind, it wasn't going to work out there. Even as he shot out lightning bursts from his dragon mouth, taking down one wave of drones after another, she knew it. He was outmatched.

And after a few good shots of his lightning breath, a round of projectiles from a large ship overhead connected, exploding all around him until one finally sent him careening to the ground. He hit with a thud, roared, and was hit again. Finally, amid all of the smoke and fire, Shrina caught a glimpse of his wings flapping, the dragon flying away in retreat. What little was left of his vampire army followed suit, a small contingent of them cut off by the incoming troops, then quickly put down.

Shrina tried to push herself up, to go after them and claim as many vampires to her side as she could, but after three steps, she collapsed. Her muscles strained to push herself back up, wings the only reason she was able to do so.

Kneeling at first, she found Trish there a moment later, helping to prop her up.

"We lost," Shrina said.

"We didn't." Trish pulled her around to stare into her eyes. "He escaped, yes, but I have hope."

"How can you?"

"I saw him. My brother, Pete... he was there."

At least that was something, though it didn't counteract the fact that Shrina had had her ass handed to her by the dragon, this Kengris. While there had been no sign of Alicia, it was true that finding Pete was a small victory. Getting him free would be another, and bring them one step closer to figuring out a way to get at the dragon.

18

TRENT, REMALD

The minute Trent made it back up to the top of the drop-off and could see the city again, he was drained. Not just in a normal energy way, but he felt like he'd been kicked in the balls and grabbed by the nostrils then dragged across a dirt field. It was more than that even, it was a feeling of total emptiness. He felt like he had before, when he'd been using his powers too much. But this, this was on a whole different level.

It was all he could do to find some rocks to sit down on. His gold armor clicking on them, he leaned back and stared up at the sky for a moment. No dragons in the sky, unfortunately. How nice it would have been to have one come along at that moment, and fly him back to the city. He had to laugh at himself, lying there wondering idly to himself which dragon would carry him high into the sky. Back home that wasn't exactly a rational man's way of thought. Even here, if anyone came across him reclining on the rock laughing to himself, they'd probably think he was crazy.

There had been a time when he actually thought he had gone crazy. It was shortly after meeting Shrina Collins for the first time, back when he first found out about teleportation tech and the super soldier program New Origins was hosting. He could still remember lying in bed looking out at the stars, wondering what other insanities must exist in the universe, the earth was so crazy. Well, now he had his answer. Though, now that he was thinking of back home, he started to wonder about his dad, how he was doing now and about how things were back on earth. Even the people who he hadn't talked to in a long time must've heard about what happened by now. He did wonder about Shrina sometimes too, and thought that maybe he wouldn't even mind going back someday and seeing her again. But not anytime soon. And even then it would only be a temporary thing, his home was here now. It wouldn't be too long before he would come back to his Feras. To be with her, Merax, Ezail, and the others. His new family now.

Pushing himself up, he remembered why he was here in the first place. Why he was sitting on this rock. He couldn't waste any more time, not when they had Wilnar's brother. That in mind, he stood and began the long trek back. The journey gave him time to think, to wonder about the way Ohklon had attacked him. He needed to set up some sort of mental defense against that in the future, to always be ready, always be vigilant. And that explosion back there... how amateurish he had been to nearly get killed by something so simple. Feras and Ezail would never forgive him if he died so stupidly. The thought put a smile to his face, images of Ezail laughing, of Feras staring at him lovingly. And just like that, he found his energy returning. His muscles reinvigorated, a sort of excitement taking over, so soon he was running again. Getting back as he labored on into the city as fast as he could.

When he was nearly at the gates, he noticed several guards escorting captives. As he drew closer, he realized he knew the captives. They were not the dissidents he'd been dealing with earlier. This was Gray, Blue, and Green.

"What is this?" He demanded.

One of the guards turned on him, rifle raised, but one of the others hissed at the first, and Trent realized he recognized this one from earlier. Trent stepped up to him, ignoring the one with the rifle, who was looking back and forth from Trent to the other guard hesitantly.

"Release them," Trent commanded.

The guard who had recognized him actually seemed to be considering this. However, he was apparently junior in the chain of command because the other one stepped forward, motioning the others to continue.

"These people were behind the attacks on the Holy City of Realt," the guard said, while the other one was offering Trent an apologetic look, but unable to do anything more.

"False." Trent stepped up toward him, fueled by his rise in energy, in spite of having run to reach this point. "Release them."

"You'll have to speak with his holiness, the Prince of Realt, on the matter. We're done here."

As the man turned to go, Trent felt that rage returning. The one that threatened to take him places he preferred not to go. Gray, however, turned his way and shook his head, and it was enough to bring back the calm.

Whatever needed to be done could take place at the palace. Out here, Trent only risked alienating himself and losing the only allies he had. Instead, he decided to stay with the guards, following them back to the palace in case there was trouble. While he didn't mind taking the argument up with the prince, he wasn't about to let these bastards hurt Gray or the other two.

"They didn't hurt you, did they?" Trent asked, jogging up next to Blue.

She shook her head, eyeing the guard nearby. The man had a scowl that said he clearly wanted to tell Trent to back off and shut his mouth, but he simply kept walking.

"We didn't resist, even told them what we were doing in the tunnels," Blue said.

"You were in the tunnels?"

"Hunting," Green chimed in. "After our interaction with you, we've been on the lookout. The second we saw movement, we charged in. Little did we know we would end up in the wrong place at the wrong time."

"Don't worry." Trent eyed the guards, determined. "This is all going to work out in our favor."

19

ESPINOZA, UNKNOWN PLANET C

I t didn't sit well with Espinoza, but he knew the others were already moving down the other side of the hill, separated from him and Ellins by an explosion, golden special forces, and the ships above. The best way to connect would be for him to follow Ellins. Other options could be risky, and the last thing they needed was to end up dead corpses for some alien government to probe and research.

They had gone down a ways, circling off to the right, staying out of sight from both the attackers and the ships above. Cutting around in their best guess of which way the others might have gone, Ellins cursed the ships above and their ability to knock out comms.

"Worst case, we storm their city and take the most powerful-looking person we can find hostage," Espinoza said, resting against a tree as Ellins knelt, sights on three golden soldiers as they darted by.

"Shut the hell up." She glanced back. "Actually, it could come to that."

"Damn. I was trying to make a joke. Cut the tension."

"In situations like this, it might be the tension that keeps us alive. Keep those eyes moving, that head swiveling."

"Yeah, of course."

She motioned them on and they were up, moving again. Before long the sounds of combat had died off, leaving the question in the air regarding what happened with the rest of the team. The worst he could think was that maybe they had already been defeated. That, however, was not a scenario he was willing to accept.

"We have to find them," he said as he pushed aside a tree branch. The vegetation had by now become denser, more like a jungle than a forest. "Agreed, and get our asses out of here alive." Ellins spun at a noise in the bushes, only to find a strange animal that looked somewhere between a tarantula and a mouse. It scurried past, hissed, and was gone. "They can handle themselves. We're still alive, my guess is they still are too." She walked ahead, but hesitated, going back to walk next to him. "And Ruan?"

He quickly explained what had happened as they walked, happy for the chance to distract his mind from their current predicament. Whenever there was silence, he imagined Kim, gunned down by aliens.

Another patrol flew by overhead, the gold soldier visible in the distance working his way between trees.

"Do you think these ones are related to the Goldies?" Espinoza asked.

"We're sure going to find out."

Feeling more positive again, they saw they needed to move through the clearing ahead, until the patrol was gone. As they did, Ellins stifled a laugh.

"Losing it already?" Espinoza asked, trying to be playful in his tone, but his worry shining through.

"Not that. It's the idea that we're out here taking a whole planet by ourselves, basically."

"Right. Exactly what I don't find funny about the whole scenario."

She grunted, then said, "Who would've thought it back home? All those officers, all those government planners. And the whole mission fell apart. Here we are, and it's up to us. Meanwhile, Ruan is out there possibly destroying or about to destroy everything we're trying to build."

"You ask me, nobody is better for the mission."

"Sure, sure." She started working her way around the clearing, once or twice motioning up to the sky and pulling back into the shadows. Finally, on the other side she said, "If the mission is to wreak havoc, we're good to go."

He chuckled at her choice of words, but his laugh was cut off as he saw a gold form move in his peripheral vision. Going to one knee he spun, lifted his blaster and aimed. Nothing there.

"Probably another one of those damn spider things." Ellins kept moving.

"I thought they looked like mice," Espinoza said. "Did you see the way the--"

Heavy footsteps, but this time when he spun, it was too late. One gold soldier plowed into him, tackling him to the ground, while the other one made a move for Ellins.

She was fast, ducking out to the side and scaling a tree. But Espinoza had been caught unawares, and even as he tried to fight back, two more soldiers appeared, dragging him off. He got off a good shot to one of them, only to find another with a hand on his face, gold pulses hitting him, putting him to sleep.

He struggled, trying to fight the sleep as one would after taking way too much NyQuil. It was no use, and soon he was fading in and out of slumber, while trying to shoot the enemy.

The next thing he knew, he was waking up beside a tree, the bag that had been strapped to his back now at his side as a gold soldier went through it. One of the ships had landed nearby. Not one of the huge ones, but one of those not much bigger than a pod. Two other soldiers were exiting the pod, moving towards him, and he tried to get up to fight them, but he found his body unresponsive.

Each wrapped an arm in his, dragging him toward the ship. Again he tried to fight, but it was no use. They dragged him into the ship as shots were fired from somewhere. More than one shot connected with the ship, and they made little noises that sounded like some form of communication. The gist of it was that they needed to move fast.

Passing side rooms, Espinoza noticed one of those soldiers sitting in what looked like one in a line of coffins of glass and metal. As they passed, he tried to get a better glance. The one next to the man, a soldier, was asleep with the glass closed. And another one beyond that had what looked like a Goldie inside.

Somehow this had to do with how they made the Goldies.

More shots were now flying through the air, actually inside the ship, one heading towards the soldier to Espinoza's right. The being stumbled away, before another shot hit it and tore open his throat. To Espinoza's left, a soldier rushed up to join them, only to be hit in the left eye with another shot. Finally, Espinoza was able to move his head and see Ellins at the entryway, ducking back to recover as the gold soldiers returned fire.

"Dammit, get your ass moving!" Ellins shouted.

"Can't..." Espinoza muttered as best he could. "They did something... I'm... Trying."

"Son of a bitch." Ellins returned fire again, then charged over and slid down behind one of the coffins by him. "You see what's in those?"

He did his best to nod, and muttered, "Making... Goldie's."

"Something like that," she replied, then had him up and lobbed a grenade into the ship as they tore out of there. His legs were starting to move as the blast hit and sent them flying. They were up again, this time changing course, moving for a small hill ahead.

"We need to get out of here, out of sight for now. Then we can find the others." Ellins motioned ahead, and for the first time Espinoza noticed the door on the side of the hill, another temple on the far side of it and mostly obstructed from view. With that as their target, they charged on.

SHRINA, VIRGINIA

No sightings of Kengris had been yet reported, and that gave Shrina hope. He had suffered his own setback, as had she. Maybe he had even been wounded, but he had definitely lost most of his troops.

Shrina and hers were back at the safehouse, lying low while Washington debated their next move and drones scoured the country in search of the dragon. For all they knew, he could have had plans to go overseas, or would hide out until he had a strategy for taking out the ship that had attacked him. There were more ships like it, after all. He had reason to be worried.

For her part though, Shrina was simply anxious. She wanted to get out there.

There was, of course, the fact that one of hers had gotten wounded. While at first, Trish had been freaking out, Irithu was, after all, a vampire. When the wound started healing and was well enough to ignore, Trish returned to her jovial self again.

"Can't you just use this strange calling power you have?" Trish waved her hand around Shrina's head as if there were some magic in there. "If we could find his location, we could send in more of those attack ships."

"It's not as simple as that," Shrina said as she went about making chicken in the safe house oven, doing it the old way her mother had done with breadcrumbs and lemons. It was only fried chicken, but it would do.

"What's up with you and the chicken anyway?" Trish asked her, looking at her askance. Shrina wondered if there was some minor reconnection going on. No, it was probably just a chicken.

"Memories?" Shrina knelt, looking at the light on in the stove, wishing it were ready. She had no idea when the next attack would come, and was damn hungry.

"I don't follow."

"You know, all the things that you used to enjoy as a child … For me it was chicken and dumplings. Fried chicken! You see the pattern?"

Trish chuckled, shaking her head. "Never was into the stuff myself. More of a steak and eggs girl, or just a good salad. When I want to reward myself, I go for Eggs Benedict."

"Too complicated."

Irithu entered then, grinning, a sling around his shoulder. "Hey, as long as it ain't blood." All three shared an awkward silence and look of disgust. "Sorry, the craving came on bad when I was healing."

"Interesting, how that works." Shrina went to the fridge, glad to see Richards had ensured they were fully stocked. She pulled out some carrots and hummus, then went to the freezer. She paused at the sight of it packed with bags of frozen, red liquid. "Blood?"

"Right…" Trish closed it for her. "He mentioned that. In case of emergencies, he said."

"For example, if I don't heal properly." Irithu pulled down the corner of his shirt, revealing his shoulder and chest. It looked pretty good, more like it had simply been scraped across the pavement versus being shot and clawed by the dragon. "I'm thinking I won't need it."

"Isn't this like keeping a bunch of drugs at a rehab clinic?" Shrina asked the other two, trying to figure whether they were resisting the urge, or even had the urge at all. Trish seemed fine, but Irithu was clearly struggling, in spite of the smile.

He shrugged, walked over to get some water, and leaned back to watch them.

"What?" Trish asked.

"Just curious to see what you all talk about when I'm not in the room."

"For that to work you have to literally not be in the room," Trish chuckled, then walked over to him and put her hand on his chest as she kissed him. Glancing back at Shrina, she added, "But we can pretend."

"Oh, sure." Shrina rolled her eyes. "We're fighting a war, but let's just talk about how amazing your new boyfriend is."

"Okay, okay, I get it." Irithu gave Trish a one-armed hug, and headed back to the other room. "The others are trying to rest, but we should probably tell them to eat soon too."

"Catch." Shrina tossed him a bag of pretzels, then the hummus. "I'll call them when the chicken's ready."

After he left the room, Trish grinned at Shrina.

"What?" Shrina asked.

"What you think of him?"

"We're not doing this."

"I decided to thank you. If not for your... allowance of fun the other day, we might never have gotten together really."

Shrina nodded. The beep of the chicken sounded and with excitement, she grabbed the heating pads, then pulled it out of the oven.

"You could just skip those you know, Trish said.

"The heating pads?"

"I mean, you'd have to heal afterwards. But you don't really need them."

Shrina laughed at that. "I'd rather not have to heal when I can avoid it."

Soon she had the others at the table—all of them gathered around like a family, eating the chicken, carrots, hummus, and whatever random things they could find. She hadn't spent much time with Reed, Luis, and Ashu, so she watched them with curiosity as they spoke about what the news was saying, how it was trying to cover everything up for the protection of the people.

"And what do you all think of that?" she asked.

They all turned to her with surprise. Apparently, she had been fairly quiet around most of them and so talking came as a surprise.

Ashu pulled her hair back, fixing it as she said, "Let the people think what they want to think. They're grown-ups."

"I don't know," Reed replied.

"You think they should keep secrets from the people?"

Reed held up his hands in mock surrender to Ashu. "I don't think the general population is ready to handle news about the dragon." His eyes moved over to Shrina, and he grinned. "Of course, a beautiful dragon such as yourself is a completely different matter."

Shrina shook her head, tapping the table. "I know for a fact, I'm not about to walk into Times Square and check out the Christmas tree next year. Going for a shopping trip at the outlet malls? Not likely. Trying to figure out how best to think about it, and what I'm leaning toward is basically a celebrity. The scary, horned, scaly celebrity."

"And still pretty." The man grinned, and laughed as Luis and Ashu threw bread rolls at him.

"No hitting on the boss," Ashu said.

"Fraternization after all," Shrina said with a wink his way..

He nodded, giving in.

Annoyingly, Trish was looking at Shrina with worry.

"Don't look at me like that," Shrina said, taking a gulp of her water.

"You don't really… I mean you know you're still beautiful, right?" Trish gulped, looked down at the table, starting to pick at her nails. "You're amazing, you're…"

"Don't you listen to a pity party for me. Don't patronize me, or whatever this is." Shrina took a bite of her chicken, letting the silence linger until she had swallowed, and added, "I believe I have a purpose now in life, and that is to kick ass."

"All cheers to that," Irithu said as he held his glass in the air.

The rest joined in, and soon they were telling stories about back home. When Trish told them about how her brother Pete had always insisted on her having a stocking for Christmas, always making sure it was filled to the brim with delicious chocolates and little toys, even well into her thirties, everyone was smiling and feeling warm inside.

"And you?" Irithu asked Shrina. "What brought you into all this?"

Shrina consider the question for a moment, moved her chicken around the plate with a fork, and then shook her head. "There's no real answer to that, is there? I can say I didn't want to sit home and do nothing, to work at a grocery store, or wash dishes. Other than that, maybe it was just an inner voice that told me to sign up. To be part of the FBI, to go bigger and better. To make the world a better place anyway," she chuckled, "Now look at me. Suppose I always wanted to be the one to bring the thunder, but never had the confidence. Now that I'm... Whatever I am... a demi-dragon, I like to think, maybe now I can."

"Well said," Trish responded, glancing around the table. "For me, it was partly my brother. Not wanting to let him be more hardcore than me. Growing up, it had always been that way, whether it was martial arts or sports. I always had to one up him. He was the type who would often say that girls couldn't do X, Y, or Z, so... I showed him. Girls can be vampires just like boys."

More laughing.

A dizziness struck Shrina, but it was external. She glanced down, thinking how she was only halfway through her piece of chicken. Then it hit again. A calling, pulling at her, and then... a voice. Not Kengris, but Alicia's.

"He's ready for you, and only you," she said, as if standing right beside Shrina, who spun, looking for its source. Shrina excused herself, and made for the bathroom. No sooner had she entered, when it came again. She glanced around, not making sense of it. All she found was another pull, this time stronger. "It's between the two of you now. Rise up, embrace it."

"Alicia, stay with me," Shrina called out in frustration. "Don't go!"

"I'm already gone."

Then it was gone. Shrina had no doubt about which way to go. That didn't mean it was the right move. She had her team, the military… but still she opted to go it alone.

Alicia was right. There was no point in getting anyone else hurt. No point in putting her team in danger. Not when she could stand against him.

Not wanting to upset the others, Shrina bee-lined for the rear exit. As she opened the door, she heard Trish calling after her, but didn't respond. She hesitated, but that was the extent of it. She didn't want to put them at risk, sure they wouldn't let her go alone.

The night air was uncharacteristically cool for this time of year. For a moment she kind of staggered along, watching the streetlights glinting off of the pavement. Then, realizing the other vampires might try to follow, she started off in a jog. Finally she couldn't take it anymore, worried that more people might see her. At least at night, she had a better chance of hiding her tracks if she took to the rooftops, flying along as close as she could without making a silhouette in the sky.

So that's what she did, following the call from Alisha. She was going to win this. One on one, or at least as close to that as she could make it.

She didn't have far to go. No sooner had she left the buildings behind and started through some trees, a force hit her and pummeled her to the ground. Pain seared, her instincts roaring to life as she struggled to get out of Kengris's grip. Her intension had been to find him, figure out a way around it, and assassinate the bastard. Of course he had made it so simple. She felt foolish now for even thinking that was a possibility.

She struggled, she realized he wasn't hitting her, just simply holding her.

"What is this?" She demanded, trying to break free.

"You must listen to me, daughter."

She wasn't ready. That moment that he had taken to reply, she struck. She managed to get her arc baton out and thrust it up into him, except for some reason the electricity hit her instead. Feeling the jolts course through her body, Shrina fought to keep her eyes open, to keep her entire focus on resisting the urge to go limp... and failed.

TRENT, REMALD

As Trent had insisted the guard bring their new prisoners to an audience with the prince immediately, nobody had dared argue. So there they were, standing in the throne room, a room Trent hadn't been to before, much more grandiose than anything he'd seen so far. This one had tall silver urns, huge vaulted ceilings with what looked like wooden beams but actually seemed to be made of silver, and murals covering the far wall. Three thrones were facing them, but remained empty for the moment.

"We just had an attack. What is the meaning of this?" The Queen demanded as she entered angrily.

Behind her came the prince, Merax, and the rest of Trent's group, along with a retinue of guards.

"Good job," Yoldrok said. His eyes went from his guards, to the captives, then to Trent. "You...?"

"Your guards have arrested the wrong people. Again."

While Yoldrok didn't seem to appreciate that, his eyes turned to the prince for the next step.

"Explain yourself," the prince demanded of Trent.

"I fought alongside these people, and can vouch for them." Trent stood tall, aware that all eyes were on him. He was a man who stuck to his guns, who was loyal to those who helped him. "Gray and his followers are on our side."

"Considering that you've only just arrived, I find it hard to believe that you know who is on whose side."

"I know what I know. I'm telling you, Gray saved my life. Blue and Green as well. We need people like this."

"Your Highness, if I may…" Gray bowed his head waiting.

"Go on." The Prince stood, waiting.

"I know those tunnels. We were hunting them, and we believed we were close." Gray turned to Trent.

Taking a hint, Trent stepped forward. "Wilnar, want to find your brother? You need them."

"I agree." Wilnar turned his attention to the Prince. "I'm taking Gray and his people. We're doing this."

The Prince looked slightly taken aback, but nodded. "If you're wrong, this falls on you."

"We won't be."

Following the Queen, the Prince exited the room. Yoldrok stood among the guards, eyeing Trent before giving him a nod and following the others out. This was his chance, but it wasn't just about him, of course. This was a defining moment, and along the way perhaps forming an alliance between the kingdom and Gray's people.

"Where do we start?" Merax asked, stepping forward and clasping hands with Gray.

"They have a lead on us now," Gray said. "But we've got this. Follow me."

No waiting around, no time spent going to the armory to buff up. Instead they took the weapons they had, and were soon out in pursuit. Before they reached the doors, however, Yoldrok reappeared.

"We'll move faster if we take one of the ships." He motioned for them to follow.

"You're coming with us?" Feras asked.

Yoldrok smiled. "I wouldn't miss it for the world."

In a matter of minutes, they'd made it, boarded the ship, and were off. Yoldroc piloted the ship, with the dragons following on behind them, including Feras and Ezail, while Gray gave directions. They flew over the first hill, back toward where the battle had taken place that Trent had been involved in.

Touching down behind the trees, far enough away from sink holes to not have to worry about that issue, they all disembarked and gathered around while the dragons transformed.

Yoldrok eyed Gray, waiting for his move, and his coming made sense—he was there to keep an eye on his 'prisoners,' to ensure all was as they said. Considering the fact that they and Merax's group weren't on the best of terms with the royal family to begin with, Trent couldn't blame the man.

"How's this going to work?" Feras asked, taking stock of the team. It was her and Ezail, Yoldrok, Merax, Wilnar, Dolog, Gray, Blue, Green, and Trent.

"We were narrowing down their area of operation," Gray began. "That led us to the point where we were captured. Since we started from here, I figured we'd go back through here and retrace our steps. From there, we have three directions to go, so I'd recommend we break it up with Feras, Green and Wilnar on one team, Yoldrok, Merax, and myself making another, and that would leave Dolog, Blue, and Trent together."

"Three teams of three," Trent said, but then glanced around, realizing the count was off. Ezail was scowling, so he put it together. "You left her out."

"I'll be expected to stand watch up here," Ezail said. "As I always am."

"To be fair," her mom said, "dragon powers aren't as helpful down there."

She had a good point, and Ezail nodded. "I get it— and chances are we're as likely to find trouble up here as down below. You can count on me."

"At least not many of the ones we've come across can shift," Feras said.

"But… there are the androids," Trent pointed out. "Is that something we should be worried about?"

"Cannon fodder," Yoldrok said with a dismissive

wave of his hand. "The enemy has them, but we aren't worried."

"Meaning our side doesn't have any?" Trent asked. "They could in theory be mass producing their soldiers, pumping them onto our planet and—"

"Our planet?" Yoldrok asked, amused but also dismissive.

"He's with us now." Feras said. Matter of fact, no question about it.

Trent felt a swell of pride at that, gave her a nod of appreciation and turned back to the others for an answer to his question.

"No, we don't have that technology," Merax admitted. "We had them before, but in the divide, anyone who knew anything about making androids left with them. I'll be the first to admit it's not an optimal situation."

"And beside the point, at the moment," Gray reminded them, indicating the nearest sink hole. "Let's move out, before our prey escapes. If it's not already too late."

So they moved on, going below ground and leaving Ezail as lookout. Trent didn't like the idea of her being there alone, but the third time he expressed his concern, Feras kind of went off about how she was a shifter, fifteen and capable of handling more than her own.

The meaning of age changed a lot when one could become a deadly dragon, Trent assumed, and let the matter rest. He focused instead on trying to pick up the scent of the enemy, of opening his mind to search for them, to see if Ohklon would try to get in there with mental attacks again. So far, nothing.

Each tunnel looked like the one before, mostly rock and dirt, with the occasional lump of roots or traces of silver among the rock. Memories of Marine Corps training flooded back to Trent. Of crawling through the mud as rounds went off overhead, of insurgent training where he and his fellow Marines would run through fake villages and tunnels very much like these. Clearing rooms, taking down the actors who were paid that day to play the enemy. It had all been very tiring and stressful, and yet, fun. Because back then, there hadn't been the reality of knowing anyone in your party could die at any moment. It had been only training.

After that, he'd had plenty of real-life experience. Real threats, real losses. People he had cared about that were gone forever.

Still, add the idea of dragon-like aliens to the mix, along with the demi-dragons who couldn't transform but were still damn intimidating, the old days didn't seem to hold up.

Gray lifted a finger, eyes darting around. In that darkness, Trent noticed something he hadn't before about the man—the way his eyes glowed light blue, almost gray. Now the name made sense, and Trent glanced back to see that Blue and Green had reasons for their names, too, related to their eyes glowing the respective colors. He frowned, looking to see that Feras and the others were using gold.

"Different colored lights?" he whispered to her as Gray moved to a wall, hand on it.

"Of course. Ours has a special purpose, as does each of theirs. Gray uses a special connection that helps in our particular case."

"Metal," Gray whispered, looking back their way as he placed his ear to the stone wall. "When it comes to being hunted, they would have been smart to not have brought androids with them. But it's more than that—there's metal in these rocks, in the soil. I can sense its vibrations, as if it's communicating with me."

Trent licked his teeth, considering the implications of this while Gray motioned them forward.

"This was the point," Gray said, as they moved up to an entrance that went on into darkness. "Beyond here, there's a larger room with the paths that diverge, as mentioned."

"What are we waiting for?" Wilnar asked, already starting to go.

Gray motioned for him to wait. "Me to tell you to be ready to fight. I think we have at least a dozen in there, though I'm not sure what they're doing. Could be waiting, setting up an ambush."

"Well then," Wilnar said with a grin—though more of a malicious grin than Trent was used to seeing on the man, "let's show them how stupid a decision that would be."

He didn't even wait for the others, but went charging in with his wings of light showing. Others cursed, but followed. Once Wilnar was in there, it wasn't like the rest had a choice. Trent stuck with Feras and Merax, the three of them entering the chamber but moving left along the wall, in hopes of flanking the enemy while their companions took them head on. As explosions lit up the room and shouts of pain broke the silence, the trio darted through the shadows. Enemy soldiers tried to take on their forces head on, giving Trent the perfect angle to send blast after blast at their sides, then the other two were behind the enemy and moved in from there.

More entered the fight, and finally Trent spotted Wilnar, wings of light visible behind him, slicing through enemy troops as he pushed a path through them to the other side.

It was all they needed, Trent's allies leading the final push to obliterate the enemy. As the last of them fell, Wilnar shouted, "Rignar!"

He ran to a dark corner of the room, where he stopped and helped a man to stand. Trent stepped closer and saw that this was the man from Wilnar's house—the brother. First step accomplished, now they needed to take the next step and take out the group that followed the High Drin.

Unfortunately, all of the enemy were dead. Having at least one alive for questioning would have been helpful. At least they had Gray. He was working around the room, checking the other tunnels while

Wilnar made sure his brother was well enough to join them. Unsteady, Rignar insisted he was.

"I'm sensing two groups," Gray said. "But that doesn't mean the third path is unoccupied. It could even be a false trail, a ruse, if they know of my skill."

"Let's assume they do, and stick to the plan," Wilnar said, letting his brother walk on his own, but watching him to make sure he was okay. "Three groups, Rignar with us."

"You're sure?" Yoldrok asked. "He could go back, keep watch with Ezail."

"I want to make these sons of bitches pay," Rignar countered, his voice firm.

Yoldrok didn't argue.

"Then it's settled," Feras said, indicating the passages. "When you've found something, be sure to let the rest of us know."

"Actually," Merax said, turning away from having been in consultation with Dolog. "I think we need to go bigger."

"The Ajargons?" Wilnar asked, eyes lighting up with excitement.

"I've sent out a call," Merax said, nodding. "They'll join us to flush out the tunnels."

"In that case…" Gray looked at Blue, and she seemed to get the message, as she turned, eyes going blue and a blue light moving across in front of her as she seemed to be typing into thin air. She finished, the light fading.

"What was that?" Trent asked, intrigued.

"Message sent," Gray said with a grin. "Our people will meet the Ajargons, so that this attack will have all we can throw at it."

"We'll start moving out," Feras said with a nod to Trent. "When they arrive, come find us. You'll be able to follow the trail of dead Exiles."

ESPINOZA, UNKNOWN PLANET C

To Espinoza's relief, they made it into this new temple, ducking in and finding, instead of an armory as before, passages. They ran along them, until they found a large open room.

Espinoza couldn't believe what he was seeing, lifting his faceplate to get a clearer view. All around, images of what looked like humans, working to pull large stones and build massive structures. It reminded him of images of Ancient Egypt, except that instead of the Egyptians serving as slave masters, in these images there appeared to be giants with wings and horns, alien creatures that resembled demons, he thought. This underground temple seemed to capture a piece of these people's history, and he was hungry for more.

Walking along the wall, he looked at images of the dragon-like statues, then dragons flying above, others coming out of the Earth.

"The sandworms," he said, voice cracking at the thought.

"What about them?" Ellins asked, approaching to look at that part of the relief as well.

"I think... See here?" He indicated a spot where one of the dragons was on the ground, wings spread to protect several sandworms. "At first I thought they were fighting each other, but this makes me think otherwise. Makes me wonder if—"

"They are connected," she replied, hand to her chin, rubbing it in thought. "It's all connected, isn't it?"

"I don't follow."

"The sandworms are like some old, long forgotten offspring from the dragons. Maybe dragons in early stages that, for whatever reason, were never able to fully develop. And the vampires," her eyes met his, "you... you have their blood. The dragon blood, it's what makes you what you are."

"No." He shook his head, then cocked in thought. "You think?"

"It's all theory, but... makes sense."

"In some sort of very 'out there' way, yes." He kept moving, but then turned back to her. "The others... maybe they'll find us here? It seems like a natural point to meet, if they're able to spot it."

"Which also means the locals are likely to think we'll come here," Ellins countered.

"Possibly." He startled, blaster ready, thinking he had heard something. After a moment, he holstered it. "Kim and Franco... I'm worried about them."

"But mostly Kim, right?" Ellins chuckled. "Don't worry, you're not the only one."

He nodded, going back to the wall, trying not to think about the others too much. Anything to distract himself.

"This must have taken them forever to carve," he noted, more to himself.

"So that we might never forget," a voice said.

Espinoza spun to see the woman from before, the one they'd been fighting with by the gate. A long weapon like a spear but with a glowing tip and a trigger shook in her hand, her eyes betraying her fear. But she stood her ground, pointing that thing at them.

"Forget?" Espinoza asked.

"Your people… coming here, befriending us, and then betraying us." She glanced over her shoulder at a distant clanging, then back at him. "How many of you are there?"

"The two of us," he replied. "Well, others back through the portal."

"At the mines," she said, nodding.

"I wasn't aware there were mines on the planet."

"The whole planet is the mines," she replied with a laugh. "The portals were established by the Apophians so that we could do their work. Their slave labor to build their—sorry, your empires. Well, it won't happen again. We've seen to that. We control the portals now."

Espinoza stared at this woman, blinking. "You're saying that you think we're these slave masters? That we are the aliens who controlled you… Is that right?"

The woman frowned, taking a step back. "No tricks now. Show your true nature. Shift so that I can see you when I put a bolt between your eyes."

Espinoza was really confused now. "And these people can shift?" When the woman didn't move or show any response, he continued. "Here's what I know. We came from Earth. Have you heard of Earth? We came through a portal, one we called the gateway to the stars. We discovered it on a planet of ours called Mars. We were attacked on our way out here, and crashed. The planet that we landed on, I believe, was the planet that we had determined via the scientists on Earth to be habitable. However, since we landed, we have been attacked left and right. By what I have started calling Goldie's, sandworms, and crazy storms. All we want to do is survive long enough for Earth to come get us. We don't know anything about Apophians, and definitely cannot shape shift."

The woman showed a slight hesitation in her eyes as she nodded toward the mural on the wall. "This here, this means nothing to you?"

"It's very interesting. It tells me that there's a culture here, a history that I'm excited to learn about. It tells me that maybe you aren't the enemy, and have only been attacking us because you see us as the enemy."

Another clanging sounded in the distance, causing the woman to startle and shoot. A bolt flew across the room, impaling itself on the center of one of the Dragons depicted in the mural, then exploded. The flash of light sent Espinoza and Ellins to the floor.

When they recovered, the woman was running out of there, her footsteps audible in the hallway. Shouting sounded, some of it in English. Confusingly, some words in a strange tongue that didn't make sense to them. Espinoza and Ellins stood and looked at each other, considering the situation. He was pretty sure she couldn't understand what the locals were saying, and if he lost the gold power, he would be in the same boat.

"We have to get out of here." Ellins said.

"But don't you see," Espinoza said, gesturing to the mural as he pushed himself up. "We don't have to fight. We aren't the enemy they think we are."

"They may not realize that anytime soon."

He knew she was right, so chose to follow her. They ran, their pursuers growing louder behind them. Soon they were sliding through passages as doors started to close. When they turned one corner, three more of those weird projectile things were aimed at them. The holders of those spears were shouting words that didn't make sense, and one woman behind them stood with arms folded, eyeing Espinoza and Ellins. This person seemed to have a position of power, as she didn't hold a weapon and her gray uniform had a very militaristic look to it.

Espinoza held up his hands. "We're not here to fight. We simply want to go home."

A shared look of curiosity among the others, and the woman in the uniform stepped forward. The others gave way to her.

"If you want to go home, then why did you come

here in the first place?" As she tilted her head, Espinoza noticed a slight glow to her orange hair. She had a good point. They hadn't come here for any other reason than to investigate her people. To see what they were up against.

"I don't mean the mining planet." He glanced back at Ellins, wondering if he was going on the right track. She gave him a nod of encouragement. "I mean Earth."

"Earth…" Her eyes roamed up, to a domed ceiling that had lines and circles drawn along it. A star chart? When she looked back at Espinoza, she said, "You're lying."

"We have no reason to. If we're part of some other force, a force sent to take you over, wouldn't I have transformed already? Wouldn't I be attacking you, trying to kill you? Wouldn't I have a whole fleet of reinforcements ready to swoop in and take you out?"

Her eyes narrowed, but she allowed a slight nod of her head.

"We don't have to have conflict here," Ellins said. "We can start a new alliance. And if that group is really out there, maybe together we can stand against them."

The woman shook her head. "Our kind will never go for it. We've been through too much, been tested, betrayed… No, it's too great a risk."

"If you'd only listen," Espinoza started, but she took a step back, hand on the wall. It lit up, a square around her hand, and then went red like it had scanned her.

"You should leave." She took another step back, eyes darting suspiciously between the two.

"We're not going to attack you," Espinoza insisted.

"At this point, she's not the one who should be worried," Ellins interjected. "Isn't that right?"

"What do you mean?" he asked.

"The gold soldiers will be here any minute, I'd guess."

The woman nodded. "Our Reshodan. The finest forces, raised for one purpose—to ensure we never become slaves again. Now leave. I prefer to not have blood spilled in my temple."

Espinoza cursed, shaking his head at the woman as he backed up to join Ellins, then the two ran for the exit.

23

SHRINA, VIRGINIA

Shrina wasn't staring at the rock walls anymore, but again she found her mind traveling through a heavy mist, clouds of orange and gold.

Remember, daughter. Try to understand...

With a jerk, she was thrust down toward the ground, where a portal shimmered blue against the mountain, three demi-dragons much like herself stepping out. Two men, one woman. All with parts of their bodies covered in scales, including their thighs, shoulders, and forearms. Broad wings, claws. They wore old-style armor, seemingly made of dragon scales, and carried swords. One stepped out from the rest, looking about, and Shrina instantly recognized him—the dragon himself. Kengris.

There was a thundering of hooves beating on the ground, and Shrina's attention was turned to the mass of riders on horseback. The army of Genghis Khan in all its glory.

"You see," Kengris said to the two with him, gesturing to this army. He stepped toward the ledge of the rocky plateau he stood on, his body and outfit changing form as he did so, making him appear like every Genghis Khan depiction Shrina had ever come across. Dragon wings were replaced with thick armor and furs, his face changing to look like the Mongolian warlord's, rounded with a wispy beard. "These are my followers, and with them I can conquer this planet."

"Kengris, this isn't the way," the woman countered.

"You can join me, you and our daughter," he said, then turned to the man. "General, we can have a life here *without* destroying this planet."

The general scowled, the woman—presumably the wife of Kengris, or at least his daughter's mother— shook her head, looking at him with disgust.

"You're starting to sound like *them*," she spat, distaste heavy in her words. "Maybe we should have just stayed put, never bothered to come to this planet at all."

"Earth," he replied. "I will take this planet, just not in the destructive way the Apophians would have it. These people have a culture we should not see burned to ashes."

"Other planets have been conquered," she replied. "Their culture still intact. Somewhat."

He clenched his jaw, then shook his head. "I won't allow it."

"My dear..." She looked at him with pity, then

stepped aside, nodding to the general. More dragon people exited through the portal. Four of them, wearing matching armor that included blackened dragon skulls at their shoulders and waists—small, as if those of child dragons.

"You bring the Horagrau against me?" Kengris growled, looking at the woman with a mixture of horror and betrayal. "

"It doesn't have to be this way," the woman replied. "You were never truly of our cause. The Apophians have seen through this, and sent me with orders."

One more of the Horagrau warriors stepped through the portal, this one with a girl in his arms, knife to her throat.

"You wouldn't…" Kengris said, almost a whisper.

"Abandon your ways," the woman said. "Step aside and let the Apophians do what we must to conquer this planet."

He gritted his teeth, hatred taking over his voice as he said, "Never."

The woman's eyes showed hesitation for a moment, but then determination. She stepped up to the daughter, taking her own blade from her belt, and turned to eye Kengris.

"No!" he shouted, lunging for her, but the general motioned and the Horagrau had Kengris pinned down in an instant. He struggled, shouting, pushing against them as the woman's blade bit into the girl's neck.

Shrina tried to look away.

Watch, daughter. Do not look away.

Daughter? Shrina wanted to shout out that she was no daughter of his, but found she couldn't reply. She was simply there, but not at the same time.

Through your death, I was reborn.

At that moment, the blade tore into the flesh, spilling blood. Steam rose in the cold air, chanting growing loud as the woman held her dying daughter, eyes gleaming red. Kengris thrust off two of the Hora-grau warriors, then snapped the neck of a third as he struggled to reach his dying daughter. The fourth gave him trouble, but ended up with his own sword through his gut, Kengris charging over to slam the general over the side of the cliff—wings flapping and saving the man, much to the surprise of the Mongol warriors below. Then Kengris was shoving the woman aside, clutching his daughter to him, blood on his hands. An anguished shout escaped his lips, eyes going to the woman who lay on her back, smiling at him.

"She's only dead in body, dear Kengris," the woman said. "You will fulfill your duty to our people. To be sure of this, your daughter won't return to you until that day. Until you have conquered Earth. You will find her, then, and bring her back from within another—with the help of this blade."

The knife was still in her hands. Others were watching, waiting to see what would happen.

I was overcome with rage, the voice of Kengris returned. *The horror of watching you die was too much.*

In the vision, Kengris laid his lifeless daughter on

the ground and leaped at the woman, quickly taking the knife and slamming it into the side of her neck. Others lunged for him, blades and claws at the ready, but he was overcome with rage, transforming fully into dragon form and snapping off heads before they had a chance to know what hit them. The general transformed as well, so that two dragons of immense size went at each other, but in the end the general retreated through the portal, taking the woman with him.

Kengris attempted to follow, but the portal closed and he was left flying off into the sky, leaving all of that behind.

I wandered the mountains for years after that. Rumor reached me of the death of Genghis Khan, who I had become. They thought me dead, though nobody ever found a body. Naturally. At least, not until many years later, when scientists of your generation discovered me in a tomb, mostly dead, and started experimenting on my body. They created a super-soldier serum from my blood, I'm told, and that started the rise of my children, the return of you, my one true daughter.

The vision faded, and then Shrina was back, only she wasn't alone. Walking toward her was a tall, proud figure. As he drew close and the light hit his features, she wasn't surprised to see that it was Kengris himself.

In his right hand, he held that same knife she'd seen him with in the vision.

"It took me some time to find the blade," he said, turning it in his hands, watching the light glimmer. "More, to find you."

"Whatever you think, I'm not that girl." Shrina tried to move, but found her arms bound. No, her entire body wasn't responding, she realized, and that terrified her. The dragon himself, Kengris, on her world a man who had taken the mantle of Genghis Khan, a warlord who had caused all manner of atrocities in his time, was approaching her and she couldn't do a damn thing about it.

"You don't understand what I've gone through to find you." He had stopped, hands held together as if praying—but with the knife held between the palms of his hands—eyes on her. "At first, I was lost. I wandered the world, taking on other forms. Hiding, confused... Even took on several lovers, protégés... slaves. You might have heard of Vlad? He made something of a name for himself. The Impaler." Kengris paused in thought, a hint of longing in his eyes, distant, but then his attention returned to Shrina. "None of it mattered, not when compared to the loss of my daughter."

"I'm telling you... she's gone."

"It must be difficult for your mind—constrained by the shackles of Earth—to understand. Our ways are not the same, and soon you will see that firsthand."

With that, Shrina was free of the mental prison that had kept her immobile. She lunged, but to her surprise, he slammed the blade into his own chest! As that had been her plan, she was left disoriented. More so when his chest began to glow, a low chant coming from his lips.

"You have my DNA," he said. "It's the reason you

have taken on this form. Many might have my DNA, but only you are the dragon reborn. My daughter, returned. Embrace your destiny."

Of course she wasn't his daughter, she told herself. She was her own person, through and through. And yet, as he started chanting again, a wave of strange images hit her, like memories flooding back. She was vaguely aware of a stream of blue light flowing from his open wound to her. Memories of another time and place, flowing backwards. That image of the mother ending her life, but from the baby girl's point of view. Horror and betrayal flooded Shrina's emotions, but then she was yanked back to a time before that even, when she was traveling through portals with her mother, marveling at holographic images of galaxies.

"These and all of the planets will be ours," her mother said, swiping her hand in a way that high-lighted several galaxies at once. "Our system of portals is established, built from the power-supplies of the Grandoix."

"And if they ever break free?" the girl had asked.

"We must not allow that to happen."

Shrina was again swept away, darkness and blue strands of light taking her to a seat in a starship, watching as Kengris was given the mission of preparing Earth. He stood tall, then, as an elder of the Apophians anointed him and said it was for the better-ment of their people, for him, and his daughter. His eyes went to her, full of love and adoration, and any hesitancy faded.

What must have happened on Earth that caused him to go against his duty? To refuse to enslave it as his people had commanded, but instead try to take over as one of Earth's people. Even to the extent that he would defy his wife as she held a knife to her own daughter's throat.

Focusing on this detail, Shrina pulled herself from the moment, gasping and falling to her knees.

"Daughter?" Kengris asked, kneeling at her side, pulling her chin up so that she could meet his gaze. "Do you see?"

"I see what happened, and who your daughter was," Shrina admitted. "But that isn't me. I'm sorry."

"No…"

"You can still be one of us." She clutched her chest, seeing the light still connecting them, but her hand going right through it. There had to be a way to break the link. "I can't be your daughter, but I can help you through this. Together—"

"No!" He pulled the blade from his chest, severing the link, and turned, running. Shrina stared after him in confusion for a moment, until she heard him call out, "Bring me the other one!"

"Alicia," Shrina muttered, realizing with horror that he was going after her sister now. He must have realized it wasn't working on Shrina, and figured he could have made a mistake on which of them the chosen one really was.

Shrina had seen the memories. Part of her wondered if there was more truth to this crazy man's beliefs than she had originally given him credit for. If so, what would it mean to Alicia if his ritual was a success?

That wasn't a possibility Shrina was able to live with.

24

TRENT, REMALD

Trent found walking through the tunnels to be quite dull when teamed up with Dolog and Blue. Blue wasn't so bad, except that most of the time she had that glow in her eyes, the weird numbers crossing her path as he imagined she was communicating back with her companions. At one point she paused, holding up a finger and muttering to herself, and then said more axis people and her own had arrived and were making their way through the tunnels.

It was nice to have the communications, though Trent preferred the Marine Corps style of simple technology. It was odd, he thought, the fact that they had the technology here but were choosing not to use it in these tunnels. Maybe, he figured, the dragons and their special light powers had ways of intercepting the communications. Regardless, Dolog was quiet most of the way, only making small grunts here and there, mostly when he thought he suspected movement ahead. They were able to sense if anyone using light skills was nearby, but otherwise it was straight up old-style tracking.

More than once, they thought they saw footprints in the dirt, but they could've been from days ago or minutes ago, there was no way of telling. A line of gold mist hovered in the air, at about eye level. Trent saw it first and called the others over, indicating the spot where it trailed into a rock. But none of them could make sense of it. So they continued on, fully aware that they'd seen something important, hoping they'd eventually find an answer even if it wasn't going to come to them yet. They would have to be patient. At one point Trent had to take a break, realizing he hadn't slept for way too long. He figured the gold light was helping him in that regard, but had to wonder about the others.

Were they all able to keep their alertness because of their powers in a world like this, where night never really came? How would they know when they needed sleep? Was it simply a matter of feeling tired and taking a rest, or did they have allotted times when they slept? He needed to know all of this eventually, but it wasn't the most pressing issue at the moment. The sounds of clashing swords and explosions, gunshots and more fighting came from somewhere in the distance. It was muffled, so they assumed it was on the other side of the stone walls, in the tunnels somewhere.

They turned to look at Blue to see if she had any information. She was going through her floating numbers, the weird blue patterns, and then finally indicated the direction they needed to take.

Dolog took the lead, and after he'd gone through several tunnels and if he started to think they were going to find the others, he'd let out a roar and charge ahead. Whenever Dolog made a sound like that, you could be fairly certain there was going to be some good action to be had.

Trent followed, with Blue at his side and together they charged out into another opening similar to the previous ones, giving a low chuckle at the encounter. Only now there were other tunnels to be seen, many crisscrossing and descending into lower caverns. Warriors were charging through, many in armor similar to that of Feras and Merax. He spotted several of the fighters from the opposing side, and when he did he charged into battle swinging and kicking, sending blasts left, right and center. They'd only been fighting for what could've been no more than a minute, when he noticed a movement in a wall nearby. He noticed it was really more like hands reaching out, and next thing he knew the strange hands were grabbing hold of Wilnar. The poor man was yanked back as purple light burst forth around him, and Trent pursued. He slid in after them even as the way closed behind, cutting him off from the others. Gold light showed in the distance, faint, and in a line. At first he turned back, trying to find a way to connect with Feras and the others, but someone had taken Wilnar and was getting away. Roars sounded, but were growing more distant, and

Trent knew he would need to move fast to catch up to them. While Wilnar could transform, the exiles had that purple-light based technology that affected the shifting and could be used to capture the shifters.

It was entirely likely that Wilnar was in big trouble, if Trent couldn't get to him in time. So he ran, charging along the tunnel and toward the gold light. He reached the light and saw that it was actually floating through the air, controlled with circles of metal bands ringed by glowing purple lights.

With each step, the golden light grew more dense until it was like a floating liquid. Trent wasn't sure how long he had been running, but finally a roar sounded close by, followed by a tremendous thud... then silence.

He turned to follow the light into a room that reminded him of a dungeon, stone walls and roof gleaming purple. Another step in, and Trent saw why. Wilnar was strapped into a mobile contraption that looked like a cot, cords with purple light holding him down and tubes stuck into him, hovering over a pool of gold water that the stream led into. The gold light from the floating stream was hovering around him, encircling him, and starting to move into his chest.

Several men and women were gathered around Wilnar, in the process of what looked like finishing applying the tubes, while two guards watched with curiosity.

Trent stood in a stupor, overhearing one of them say, "It damn-well better work, or they'll have our heads."

"We didn't do all this for nothing," another answered.

A guard looked back as he said, "It's ready."

Next thing Trent knew, one of the women had flipped a switch. Wilnar's body started shaking, the light flooding through him to those wires and an area on the wall. Now that Trent's attention was directed there, he saw that it was a flat piece of stone, different from the rest, and that it started to crumble as purple light formed around it, the gold light flooding the stone like pummeling water.

Then it was gone, and in the stone's place was a shimmering light that rippled like water. It morphed into an image of stars, a planet in the distance.

"It's done," one of the guards mouthed, his voice an awed whisper.

"We did it," another replied.

Trent had seen enough, as all of this suddenly made sense to him. They had taken Wilnar's brother for a purpose, but that purpose was now being fulfilled by Wilnar himself. Somehow, they were siphoning off his light and shifting power, funneling it into this device that opened a portal. One of the old portals that Ezail and the others had told him about, he guessed.

Opening such a portal meant the enemy was closer to bringing back the Exiles than anyone on Remald seemed to realize.

His first move was to disconnect the device, throwing himself at the cables that were connected to Wilnar's body, regardless of what that did in terms of letting his guard down. He managed to crash into them, grabbing Wilnar and rolling into the gold water as guards and the others in the room reacted slowly in confusion. By the time Trent had regained his footing and lifted his hands for a fight, they had guns aimed at him and were shouting—the portal was down.

"Enough!" one of the men shouted, and Trent wasn't surprised in the slightest to see that it was the High Drin himself. He recognized the man from when he'd been taken to the Drin's castle by Yalanov. Something this important couldn't be missed by the likes of him.

"I'm not letting this happen," Trent said, clinging tightly to the unconscious Wilnar at his side.

"It's already happening," the High Drin replied with a wicked grin. "Even as we speak, those inside of the city are rising up. Some of your greatest warriors are in the hills, and the city will fall. With the portal opened, our gods shall return to us. And you won't be able to do a damn thing about it, because you'll be dead."

He nodded, causing the guards to open fire. Blasts tore through Trent. With the impact, he fell backward into the gold liquid, pain tearing through his body. The shots had certainly hit their mark, and he felt his life force draining fast. A coldness took over as blood seeped out of him, and yet, he felt the warmth of the gold liquid surrounding him. Those idiots had shot him right into a pool of the magic that both healed him and made him more powerful. The liquid entered the holes in his body and he was overcome with a sense of completeness and self-awareness.

His eyes opened to take in the gold liquid surrounding him, almost like a mist in the sense that it didn't feel as dense as water and he was able to breathe in it, albeit a little strained. Muscles feeling the burn like after a good workout, he was overcome with the urge to shout out with excitement, to leap up and let out a loud, "Whoop!" So he did.

Bursting out of the liquid, Trent charged into the enemy, whooping some more and laughing, now more powerful than he could ever have imagined before. Each punch landed with enough power to send his opponents flying into the far walls, pain only fueling his rage and excitement. A glance down showed the wounds healing, armor covering up healed skin, and his armor became reinforced to the extent that he would even grow spikes when he struck. One of the guards attacked but got a backward elbow to the skull, one that resulted in a spike shooting out and tearing through the man's head, retracting a second later to let him fall dead to the ground. Others saw this, saw their companions who were slumped to the ground on the far walls, and they wisely started to flee.

All but the High Drin, who shouted after them, calling them cowards and threatening their lives if they didn't return.

"Don't you understand what we've done here?" he spat at Trent, only the two of them left now, aside from Wilnar who was pulling himself out of the gold liquid.

"The Exiles will come. We know how to open the portal—it's been tested!"

"Except I won't let you."

"You can't stop me, you pitiful human." He scoffed, looking Trent up and down. "What? You think this is power? You haven't seen power yet."

"Show me then. Let's find out what you're made of."

"Not me." The High Drin glanced back at the wall, teeth grinding. "But in the meantime, why not?"

He lunged, smiling as his eyes glowed red. As Trent braced himself, the room spun and Ohklon's laughter filled his mind, followed by crippling pain that shot through his body. It sent him to his knees, where the High Drin connected with an elbow to the face that sent Trent onto his back. Staring up at the ceiling and trying to regain his bearings, an image appeared, a vision of Ohklon grinning at him, then motioning to others as he transformed into a dragon and descended on the city of Realt. Guards came out to meet him, but others followed Ohklon—enough to cause some of the guards to step back with worry.

The stomping of the High Drin's foot on Trent's face brought him momentarily back to the fight, then again and again, but the gold was keeping him in one piece and not allowing such an easy beating. Trent reached up to block the next one. He caught his opponent's leg and rolled, bringing the High Drin down, but when he went for the punches he could only hit clouds of red that suddenly filled his vision.

"What's happening?" Trent asked, but even as the

words left his lips, he knew it was Ohklon. That damn blood bond was still in place. So he went for plan B, calling out, "Wilnar!"

A grunt came in response, then more fighting that came in bursts and glimpses. But Trent suddenly wasn't there at all. Instead, he was in the castle, sitting on a throne. Glancing up, he stared in confusion as Feras and Ezail charged in, both shifting to dragon form and flying at him, fire exploding out from their mouths. He dodged out of the way, came up shouting for them to stop. They didn't, though, and came back for another burst.

He knew this couldn't be real, but didn't know how to fight it. A good shot of flames melted the throne he had been sitting on, and then both of them had tackled him, transforming back, and laughing.

A laugh escaped his own mouth, too, though it didn't make sense to him, but it was followed by a gasp. Then a sob. Ezail was rolling off, a large spike protruding from her chest retracting back into his armor.

"What have you done?" Feras said, staring at him with hatred, then running to her daughter.

"It's... not me," he mumbled. "Part of... the attack on my... mind."

"This isn't some bullshit dream!" she countered, cradling her dying daughter.

Trent focused though, breathing heavily in and out, to find the truth. Then, with a jolt, he was awake.

25

ESPINOZA, UNKNOWN PLANET C

Exiting the temple, Espinoza and Ellins came face to face with one of those damn soldiers. The Reshodan, as the woman back there had called them, had his cloak billowing out behind him, a sort of ball in his hand with two curved ends on either side that glowed when he pointed it at the Marines.

"Move and you die," he said.

"Ditto," Espinoza replied, with his concealed blaster now out in one hand, taser punch with the other.

"Ditto?" Ellins asked, not quite glancing his way but kind of nodding his way. "That's your threat?"

Espinoza shrugged. "Gets the point across."

The Reshodan growled, aiming this time at Ellins. "Both of you, lay down your weapons. You will be taken in for questioning, or join your friends in death."

"Death…?" Espinoza repeated the words as if in a daze, a burning rage coming over him at the idea that this man might have killed the others. Without so much as planning his move, he was on the guy, knocking the weapon out of his hand and slamming a fist up into his gut—stunner sending him flying back. Two more Reshodan appeared around the hill, though, and while Ellins fired at them, she shouted for him to move back to the doorway.

Espinoza heard her, but wasn't thinking straight enough to act. Instead, he was on the first soldier again, going for another punch. These soldiers weren't street brawlers though, and when Espinoza came in for the strike, the man was ready. He had pulled out another weapon from his side, and rolled over, thrusting it up. A thin blade—fiery hot—extended, as if from the side of a baton, piercing armor and slicing through Espinoza's forearm.

Shock hit first, a numbing adrenaline leaving him in a state of annoyed confusion as the next moves seemed to come slower than could be possible. The blade retracted, the man aimed again, and another thrust sent the blade up and toward Espinoza's neck. As he pulled back, he tried to knock the blade aside, but it tore through his armor again, leaving another wound on that same forearm.

This time, as the third strike came, Espinoza remembered himself and shot with his blaster—a point-blank shot to the face. The man's nose came off along with part of his cheek, and then he was up and grunting, with teeth bared, looking like some Halloween monster.

Each strike that came after that was faster and

harder than the one before, but at least Espinoza was on the move, keenly aware of the shots from the other two—one that pinged off the body armor covering his calf. Ellins was at the door, but it wouldn't open this time. She cursed, returned fire with enough gusto to send the advancing two Reshodan diving for cover, then motioned to the city.

"We need a cover!"

She was right, and while most of the city was a ways off, several small huts that dotted what appeared to be farms were within reach.

"Where are their corpses?!" Espinoza demanded, now turning the fight around on Noseless, pushing the attack.

"Corpses?"

"My friends... they aren't dead?" He froze, confused. That nearly cost him an eye as the guy attacked again.

"Not yet, but my brothers will surely have dealt with them by now, I imagine."

As if in response, more shots rang out, but this time from behind the advancing two. Apparently, the guy was wrong. There, running down the hill and toward them, were the three unmistakable forms of Marick, Franco, and Kim.

"Go," Espinoza told Ellins, nodding toward the village. Then he lunged forward, catching the soldier's forearm and turning it back on himself as the blade extended. A good slice into the man's neck followed, causing him to take his own life. "That was for making me think the worst had happened, you son of a bitch."

He dropped the body, shot up at the two remaining Reshodan, while at the same time scooping up the strange weapon the man had dropped. He then turned to join Ellins behind the cover of the hill.

"Cover fire," she said, indicating the hill. "Until the others get to us."

"Not a problem." He had a blaster in one hand, the Reshodan's weapon in the other, and started firing. Two blasts, and then one from the new weapon—but as soon as he squeezed it to shoot, he collapsed, completely drained. Amid wheezing gasps for breath, he croaked, "Problem!"

Ellins cursed and helped him up, pulling him back out of the firing zone. "What happened?"

"I tried their weapon—bad move."

"Lesson learned." She pulled up his facemask, checked his eyes, then pressed on the side of his helmet to bring up his vitals. "Holy f…"

Her words were cut off by a ship flying overhead, more Reshodan dropping not far off. Shots hit the building nearby, and she grabbed him, pulling him back and over with her as she rolled out of the way.

"You need to feed," she said, already undoing her vambrace.

"I'm not… hungry." But he was, and he realized it the moment the words came out. Not for food, but for something else. For blood.

And judging by the way she was lowering down to

him, that's exactly what she had meant. Bare forearm to his mouth, she nodded.

"That's not going to happen," he muttered.

"Shut up and drink." Pressing her flesh to his lips, she flinched as more shots went off. "That's an order."

"Forget it. Not happening."

"Espi... please."

Another shot, and she lifted her faceplate so he could see her eyes. He couldn't resist the pleading there, the caring way she worried about him. He would drink, but just enough to get his vampiric healing in order.

Staring into those beautiful eyes, light brown with hints of green around the edges, he opened his mouth around her flesh. She winced slightly as his teeth punctured her skin, but then looked almost orgasmic as he started to drink of her blood. It flowed into his mouth, some trying to escape. He pressed his lips to her to catch it all, body instantly replenished by the healing life force she had given him.

Another shot—this one sending stone debris raining down on them—reminded him that they needed to get moving, and that he needed to stop drinking before it consumed him and he wouldn't be able to stop.

When he pulled back, her super-soldier healing was already causing the blood to clot, the skin to heal. She gave him a nod, quickly replacing the vambrace, and said, "How's it feel?"

"Oddly passionate."

"Shut up." She gave him a smile and a wink, closed her faceplate, then his. "We need to connect with the others."

"Take out the closest soldiers, then get to the huts."

"Exactly."

As one, they were up and charging. They moved around the hill and, rejuvenated, Espinoza moved like the wind, cutting through the terrain and leaping over enemy blasts as his own shots connected. One of the Reshodan dropped, giving Espinoza a clear view of more of them firing to the left beyond—where he assumed Kim and the others were. Shots from Ellins distracted the second Reshodan, giving Espinoza the chance he needed to clear the distance. A moment later, he was on the man and slamming him to the ground. Two shots to the face, then a couple of stomps for good measure.

Then they were off to join their friends.

26

SHRINA, VIRGINIA

The hallway was dark, each footstep echoing between shouts from the dragon.

"Not her!" Shrina shouted, charging after the man. "Stay away from my sister..." The last bit was little more than a whimper.

The dragon had left her sight, replaced by four vampires moving toward her. And walking with them, was a man she had once been curious about, but now loathed. But this wasn't the same Cody as before, he had transformed. With horns growing from his head and arms, ears pointed and eyes red, he was fully decked out in an exoskeleton complete with blue glowing energy sphere at his chest. In one hand, he held a baton that had a line of the blue glowing light running along it, and in his other hand he held a pistol with a similar energy source.

"Can't stop it now." He lifted the pistol, aiming it at her. "But it doesn't have to be this way. My uncle once had a vision for us, and I see that future now. I see it clearly--you will be by my side as I rule this world in the name of the Apophians."

"The what?" Shrina didn't really care what he was saying, but was looking for a way to buy time, to plan an attack.

"The people that Kengris belonged to. He means to return with his daughter, to regain his seat of power. He will rule from above, with me as his proxy here. Together, you and I can repopulate this earth. Not just the Apophians' own offspring, though of course that will happen. No, we will transform the population. Our army will take control, as many have already begun to do. We have people in strategic positions of power as I speak, making moves to overthrow those in charge. This is a new world, Shrina, help me to forge it."

"Not gonna happen."

She found her opening, slicing through the air with wings back, coming up for the punch, her wings forward to slam two of the men back into Cody. Cody got a shot off, but it tore through one of his own men. The blast removed part of his head as if it was thrown into another dimension. Cody let out a growl and came at her with the baton, air sizzling is it passed by, inches from her face. She had one advantage here, and that was that she didn't need to fight him. She needed to get to the dragon, to her sister.

Only, as she flapped her wings and moved away from him, turning to throw herself into the hall where she believed the dragon had gone, a blue light flashed and Cody appeared directly in front of her.

"Your choice is made." Cody shook his head, sadly. "Maybe in another life."

This time when he shot, he didn't miss. She was able to throw herself to the side, but hadn't allowed for her wings. A blue blast tore through the bottom section, leaving her grunting with pain. But he hadn't realized just how fast she was. Before he could get off a shot she had pushed through the pain and was on him. He had full body armor on, and it wasn't until her horns dug into his flesh, then pulled out, that he was left screaming in agony. He would heal, if he truly was one of them, but not right away. That was enough.

She slammed her forearm into his, ducking under to the outside of his arm and slamming his hand that held the pistol. Pulling herself free from his grip, she let one of the horns from her wings tear into his neck as she slipped outside of his area of attack. With a good roll, she was up and into the next hall. Two shots back, and then she saw what she was looking for. She slammed her hand on the control panel, closing the door between herself and him.

The last she saw of Cody in that moment was of him staggering toward the closing door, blood dripping and sizzling in an acidic way as it touched the floor. The door was closed, and he wasn't a threat anymore.

Only a couple more turns, and then Shrina found two guards. With her strength and speed, they were no problem. She was too late. By the time Shrina had fought through the guards, she entered to see Alicia hovering off of the ground with wings of blue light, eyes flaring blue as well, and she reached out for her father's embrace.

The two hugged, father and daughter reunited. Only, that was Shrina's sister—not this lunatic's long-lost daughter reincarnated, or whatever insanity he was espousing.

"Alicia!" Shrina shouted, slamming her shoulder into the glass door and sending a spider web of cracks through it. The second strike sent her tumbling through the glass as it shattered, then she was up with wings outspread, claws at the ready, and threw herself at Kengris.

It wasn't the man that she found herself fighting, but Alicia. A few good strikes, and then Shrina was thrown back, landing on the ground. There she sat, staring up in confusion as Alicia knelt before Kengris, head bowed.

"You have proven yourself, and I promise, daughter." Kengris stepped toward Alicia, taking her chin in his hand. "You come first. Never again will I balk in my duties. Never again will I put you at risk."

The blue flared and her attack on Shrina returned with vigor. Alicia was unlike anything she'd ever been, the light started to merge with her so that the wings were now growing out of her, part of her flesh. Horns developed as well, and Shrina saw herself in her. No matter how many attacks came Shrina's way from Alicia, though, Shrina wouldn't strike back.

"This isn't you," Shrina shouted between blocks and dodges. "You have to fight this, push him away. You're not his daughter."

"How little you know..." Alicia managed to grab hold of Shrina by the hair, pull her down with a strike to the throat.

That left Shrina stumbling back, gagging for breath, one hand out to try to stop her sister from advancing. Alicia's wings spread out and she leapt into the air before diving for another attack. This one was a kick to the stomach, followed by a good punch to the face. She wasn't actually trying to kill her, it seemed. More... Defeat her. Leave her broken. A glance at the dragon, the way he was smiling, showed this to be a possibility. And if so, maybe Shrina could use it to her advantage. At least, it would keep her alive long enough to think of a way out of this.

A door opened up nearby, and Cody and two of his vampires charged in. The man looked somewhat healed, but with chunks of his left side missing. Must have been where her shots had connected. The three moved up behind her, blocking her from any route of escape. In front of her was Alicia slightly to the left, and past that, more to the right, stood Kengris.

"The world will never be the same," Cody said. "There's no use fighting it."

"Then I'll die trying."

"Such a waste." Kengris held up a hand, and Alicia

paused in her attack. Stepping forward, the man's eyes roamed from sister to sister, settling back on Shrina. "My daughter is returned to me. I have no use for you, but you love her. Deep down, there is still a part of her that loves you, too. You have a choice now, join us, or watch as my daughter tears you limb from limb."

"Your daughter died long ago."

Kengris clearly didn't like that, eyes flaring red, and the two vampires flew at her as if he had thrown them from the other side of the room. Shrina dodged aside from one, slamming his face in the ground, while the second caught her with a good hook to the chin. She was about to counter, when Alicia was on her again, picking her up and throwing her into the wall. Slamming face first into metal never felt good. Shrina rolled just in time to avoid a heel from one of the vampires, then caught his leg and twisted so that she stood and broke it. Pulling the man, she used him as a diversion, tossing him at Alicia, and then charging and going for her legs. It worked, and a moment later she had Alicia on the ground. She didn't strike, but fell, arms tight in an embrace as she whispered into the woman's ear, "You are Alicia. You are my sister, now and forever. Remember our family, remember Prestige... And remember Marick."

The blue faded from Alicia's eyes, and for a moment she looked at Shrina with worry and hope. "Get me out of here."

"Stay with me," Shrina replied, starting to pick her up, only to find the blue returning.

In a flash, Alicia was grabbing her, pulling her down to an open mouth with sharp teeth at the ready.

"Focus!" Shrina grunted, pushing away. "Marick, Prestige, focus on—"

A thud sent red and black into her vision, knocking her sideways and onto the floor. She tried to get back up, but saw Cody there with his baton crackling, took a swing to the face, and fell again.

Lying there in pain, moaning, she was vaguely aware of Kengris and Alicia walking off.

"Finish her," Kengris said. "I was wrong about her. She's no longer needed."

"Alicia…" The words barely escaped Shrina's lips before another strike landed, then the other two vampires were on her again, beating her to shit.

"Enough." Cody took one of their guns, standing over her, and opened fire. She had enough time to roll, wings deflecting the shots as she recovered the pistol from him.

One well-placed shot and there was a hole where Cody's eye had been, a clean hole that went straight through to the back of his head. His mouth fell open and the other two looked at him, watching as his rigid body fell backward to the ground, where it went limp.

Two more blasts, took down each of them in turn.

Shrina pushed herself up to one knee as she holstered the weapon as best she could in her uniform, pain shooting through her ribs and across her right cheek. Bones were undoubtedly broken, but they would heal. What wouldn't heal, if she didn't deal with it immediately, was the situation with her sister.

As far as she knew, the longer Alicia was with the dragon, the more lost she was. There was no doubt that his magic had worked, at least on some level, and was bringing something out in Alicia that hadn't been there before. Whether it was in any way related to the man's daughter, Shrina had a hard time weighing in on.

With one last look at the fallen form of Cody, Shrina cursed and then ran, stumbling out of there, in pursuit. The connection between her and Alicia, even with Kengris, was still strong. Following them wouldn't be difficult.

The question of what she would do once she caught up with them was the troubling part.

27

TRENT, REMALD

"We need to get back to the city," Trent muttered, coming out of it in time to see the High Drin overpowering Wilnar, starting to push the man back into the contraption that had opened the portal.

Muscles screaming in protest, hot pain in places where he had been struck while out of it, Trent managed to roll over to his hands and knees. It took all of his energy to throw himself at the High Drin, just as the portal opened again. The High Drin stumbled into it, grasping for the metal siding, and cursed with a thrust of his hand that sent blue and purple blasts at Trent. The blasts bit into the stone behind Trent as he dodged, and he countered with a blast that drew from the nearby liquid and sent a solid punch of gold at the man.

It hit, knocking the High Drin's hand loose from its precarious hold on Wilnar, and then he was gone, off into space of some other galaxy or system or who the hell knew where. Meanwhile, Trent pulled Wilnar free again, and this time called on his powers to smash the cot-like device they'd used to drain him, and sent the pieces through the portal as it closed.

He supported Wilnar with an arm under his shoulder, and together they stepped back into the liquid. Both healed rapidly, so that they were stepping out when others came through the hole that the blue and purple blast had created.

"Hold," Trent demanded, ready to blast apart any enemy that came through.

To his enormous relief, it was Feras and, surprisingly, Ezail. They were eyeing the pool and rest of the room with confusion.

Trent stared at Ezail, unable to believe his eyes. "I— I thought you were dead."

"What...?"

"Nothing. It's not important." He stepped forward and wrapped his arms around her, feeling that she was indeed alive and breathing. With a laugh of relief, Trent turned to Feras and kissed her.

"Oh." Ezail stared at them with wide eyes. "It's like that now, is it?"

"It is," her mother said, taking Trent's hand.

Ezail nodded, but seemed troubled.

"Is that okay?" Trent asked.

She took a moment, then smiled wide. "Better than okay. Just... wow. I never knew if my mom would learn to love again."

Trent and Feras shared a caring smile.

"Wait, weren't you supposed to be keeping watch?" Trent asked Ezail.

"Figured she would do better down here," Feras said. "Once all the troops started showing up."

"The troops, right—the city, it's under attack!" Trent was already moving for the exit when Feras spun him around.

"How do you know?" she asked.

"I saw it—Ohklon was practically bragging."

"Or… filling your mind with false images." She glanced around, eyeing the gold pool, then the far wall behind it. Oddly, the pool seemed to be swaying but not slopping against the wall. "I wonder…"

An explosion rocked the room as she entered the pool, then another as she pressed against the far wall. Sure enough, it wasn't there at all, the wall had been an illusion. She motioned for them to follow, and then she, Trent, Wilnar, and Ezail stepped through.

There, at the back of the underground throne with his hand on its side and eyes on the ground, stood Ohklon. "Is it done? Has the message been sent?"

"Oh, we've sent a message," Trent answered.

Ohklon's eyes shot up to meet his, then roamed over the others. "Impossible."

"Is it?" Trent shook his head, stepping up and focusing on his breathing in case the man tried another mental attack. He would be ready this time. "Thing about people like you—you always lose out to your own hubris."

"And people like you always say stupid bullshit." He reached down to the side of the throne, drawing a blaster that he used to shoot at the one he must have assumed to be the weakest of them—Trent. However, Trent still had the reinforced armor and effects of having just been in the pool of light. The shot hit and bounced right off him, scorching the ground at Ohklon's feet.

Roars of battle sounded not far off now, then two of Ohklon's exiles charged in, only to be shot down. Some of the Ajargons followed, including the rest of Trent's friends, even Yoldrok.

As Ohklon's eyes roamed over them, then back to the blaster shot in the stone at his feet, he snarled.

"I've made contact. The true gods will soon return, and when they do… you'll all be ground to dust beneath our feet."

"But you won't live to see it," Merax countered, stepping up to fight the man.

Ohklon smirked, dropped the gun, and held up his hands. "You wouldn't."

"No," Merax said. "I wouldn't. Still…" He looked around the room, eyes landing on Yoldrok. "What's his punishment?"

"Should the Exiles arrive, we might want him as a bargaining chip," Yoldrok replied. "As much as it pains me to say it."

"And the city?" Trent asked, not liking one bit that this man would stay alive.

Yoldrok turned to Gray, who in turn eyed Blue. She

checked, then nodded. "A small rebellion, but nothing the royal family can't quell. That said, if they had help it could avoid higher casualty rates."

"Bring the prisoner," Yoldrok commanded, though it wasn't clear who he was telling since nobody there technically worked for him. Still, they obliged. "Let's go end this little uprising."

ESPINOZA, UNKNOWN PLANET C

With the ships raining down fire and the various Reshodan in the hills, meeting back up with the rest of the group wasn't going as smoothly as Espinoza had hoped. Even with the blood he had drunk flowing through him, he was at most moving slightly faster than before. Lesson learned—don't play with alien toys without knowing how they work. His bet now was that they used some of that gold energy, drawing it from the user. Since he had been so low on gold power at the time of attempted use, it had nearly crippled him.

Thank God for Ellins.

A glance back as he ducked into a ravine showed her keeping up fairly well. As far as he could tell from her movements, he hadn't taken too much of her blood. Not enough to make her woozy, at least. More ships zoomed in, but they stayed out of sight until the sky was clear again, then they were up and charging.

"Where the hell are they?" Ellins grumbled, the fighting having apparently hit a lull. No shots were heard, and the Reshodan couldn't be seen.

"Last we saw, this way," Espinoza replied, pushing toward the closest tree line.

Halfway there, though, an explosion hit the bottom of the hill, followed by a shout, then more shouts. Reshodan appeared out of the treeline, charging in that direction. And there, hobbling away from the blast zone, was Marick!

"Go!" Ellins shouted. "I'll be right behind you."

They darted out, eyes to the sky as ships appeared coming over a hill. Maybe they had seen the runners, maybe not. Faster they ran, as the ships started to turn around. Espinoza had no doubt that once those ships started firing, there wasn't much chance his armor would hold up.

An explosion went off to his right and he turned to see a Reshodan falling, then Franco stood up and shouted, "Get some!" before firing what looked like an alien rocket launcher up at one of the ships.

It hit, and emitted a sort of electronic explosion that then caused smaller explosions around it, similar to fireworks that branched out. The shot did its job, sending one of the ship's engines into flames. Steering wildly, the ship hit the one next to it, and a cheer rose up from Kim as she pulled at Franco, the two of them running with Marick toward the huts.

"Yo!" Espinoza shouted, wishing comms worked.

Ellins was with him a moment later, both speeding

toward their group and finally connecting by a clump of rocks halfway to the hut. Behind them, one ship crashed into the side of a hill, while the other recovered.

As the remaining ships came back around, Ellins motioned to the huts. "Let's hope these guys don't bomb their own people."

From the first hut, a Reshodan emerged, shouting orders. He was followed by two locals with those alien double shooters. Another group came out to the left.

"You deal with these," Ellins shouted to Marick, then motioned to Espinoza to follow her to deal with the others.

A round object flew through the air, glowing gold and then flashing red.

"Down!" Ellins called, leaping and tackling Espinoza, rolling with him into a ditch. Kaboom! The explosion shook the ground and sent dirt and rocks raining down on them as the two stared at each other through their HUDs.

"Thanks," he muttered.

"Show your appreciation by killing those jackasses."

He chuckled as she rolled off of him. Leading the charge, it was his turn. He took one of the cylinders he had stowed in his armor from earlier and tossed it— mid-air it went off, but instead of exploding, it pulled at its surroundings. Two soldiers were sucked into the air to it, and left struggling until two shots took them both out and they went limp a second before the weapon released them with a crushing sound.

By then, he and Ellins reached the rest, opting for hand-to-hand combat. They quickly tore through the group, leaving a couple unconscious with the shock punch. As the ships were still incoming and Marick's group was out of sight, Ellins led him to the cover of the huts. Alarms could be heard from the city in the distance, and movement visible, likely more troops coming from the walls.

Separated from the other group and wanting to stay low, Espinoza and Ellins moved from the huts, crouching, weapons at the ready. They couldn't stay long, not with all the action going on around them. Before long, they would be overrun, and then it would be all over for them. Defeat was not an option.

"Over here!" Kim hissed, and Espinoza leaned out around a stone fence to see her with Franco, helping the injured Marick. Coming down the street were two Reshodan, weapons ready and eyes searching the surrounding buildings.

Espinoza held up a hand to Kim, then leaned back to Ellins, telling her about the situation. "When they pass, we make our move, ambush them before any others see, then run across to Kim."

"Good plan," Ellins said, holding something in her hand. "Or we can…" She went back to the corner of the hut, leaned over, and chucked it. A moment later, the clanging sounded and she motioned for him to go as she ducked past him, then out into the street and across.

By the time he reached the street, the soldiers were

gone, apparently having fallen for the trick. Amateur, he thought with a chuckle, and followed Ellins.

A moment later, they were ducking into the hut with Kim and the others, all reunited again.

"Is it bad?" Ellins asked Marick.

"I'll heal," he replied. As he wasn't wearing the same armor as the rest of them, the explosion had sent large burn marks up his right side, clothing missing in spots along his leg and right midsection. Burnt skin showed red and black.

"You can feed." Ellins glanced down at her arm, but Espinoza cleared his throat, not sure how he felt about her becoming the common bloodbag.

"I'll be fine," Marick insisted, as Franco stepped up, possibly about to offer himself up for the blood sucking. "First things first, we need to get to one of the portals. That one we were at, though… it's gone."

"And we don't know how to activate them," Kim pointed out.

"I do," Espinoza said. When they all turned to him, he indicated the wall nearby, where several of those gold stones were arranged. Some glowed more than others, giving off a bright light as if they were on display. "Those right there. With positions on the gate. Same way the soldiers—Reshodan—fuel their armor. And I saw something before, on one of their ships, that gives me a hint of how the Goldies are formed."

"Get the stones," Ellins said, nodding to Franco and Kim, who were closest.

They had gathered the top row of the brightest

ones, when a door creaked open. All turned at once, weapons at the ready.

"Ah, shit," the woman from before said. Kim glanced over at Espinoza, likely wondering what the woman had said, but it wasn't important.

"We're not here to hurt you," Espinoza said, the team starting to move out the door, gold stones in tow. "All we want to do is go home."

The woman eyed him with uncertainty, but didn't move to intervene. Outside, they realized why. A team of enemy soldiers and locals stood there, debating with each other in hushed tones. Not one of them saw the team until they were all outside in the open, their weapons aimed at the back of the soldiers.

"We come in peace," Espinoza said.

"All you have to do is put your weapons aside," Ellins added. "We won't hurt anyone. We just need to get to one of those gates, open it and get back to the other planet."

"Peace?" an older woman with green, glowing hair said. She scoffed. "You don't get to say that." She motioned to her followers, who went into one of the huts, returning a moment later with a figure dragged between them. "Not after this."

The others threw the figure on the ground, but Espinoza knew it was Ruan before he could see her. She looked like hell.

"Dammit," he muttered, turning to Marick and Ellins. Judging by the look in their eyes, they agreed that his hopes of finding a way to peace with these people was gone. Not that they had much of a choice in the matter, though. That choice was made when the locals had decided to torture Ruan.

And torture her they had.

Even as her skin started to heal, Ruan lay there with her blood seeping out from open wounds. Flesh was clearly mending, but it would take a damn long time. Parts of her were even hanging off, and it was unclear whether those bits would heal at all. Espinoza couldn't imagine anyone living through such pain.

"You shouldn't have done that," Marick muttered, Ellins already looking around for exit points and additional threats.

"Is that right?" the strange woman asked. "You come to our world and tell us what to do with those who would see us dead?"

"There's no going back now," Espinoza said, and he was already pulling out the rest of the arsenal he had been able to conceal, lobbing a grenade at the soldiers as he fired, Ellins shooting next, then the others. Marick ducked out of sight, coming out a moment later from a doorway down the way, catching one of their soldiers off-guard and sinking his teeth into the man.

Good call, too, because that scream of terror sent some of the locals into a frenzy. Also, the blood left Marick in ultra-soldier mode, moving faster and attacking with more ferocity. There was no worrying about killing or not here, because the locals had made their position clear. Maybe Ruan had instigated the fight, an idea that Espinoza had no problem believing, but their reaction and attack couldn't be interpreted in any way other than aggression.

Espinoza saw Kim in trouble so ran to her, slamming a soldier into a wall before blasting him up through the bottom of his neck and into his head. Next, he spun to see Kim giving cover fire while Franco charged forward, then Franco shouting for her to leap-frog through the area.

"There!" Marick shouted, running past them and indicating a gateway near the huts, at the base of another hill. Past it, a small waterfall created what might have otherwise been a little spot of paradise.

Espinoza repeated the instructions, already moving for the gate when a Reshodan leaped from a building and knocked him over with a double-kick to the back. Shots hit his armor, one tearing through at the shoulder, but then Espinoza was up and returning fire at the same time that Kim caught the attacker with a shot from the left.

"I got you, boo," she said, charging over.

"Ah, so sweet of you. Saving my life is always my favorite gift."

She laughed as they ran together, then gave cover fire while Franco caught up, the other two coming around from the right, carrying Ruan now. Clear, the group formed a wedge and went for it, Ruan was stumbling along on her own, turning and shouting about revenge.

"Get your ass through that portal!" Ellins shouted, while Kim and Franco moved to apply the stones.

Slurring her words, Ruan stumble back toward the enemy, pulling her blaster from her hip. "Not leaving a soul alive. These sons of bitches have to pay, they—"

Ships appeared overhead, blaster shots tore through Ruan like fire through a paper doll, leaving her a smoking corpse full of holes. A pile of meat, collapsing to the ground. There was no healing from that.

"Move it!" Franco shouted. He and Kim had figured out the gate, and the portal was activating.

Espinoza nodded, crossed his heart, and turned to follow the others through.

29

SHRINA, VIRGINIA

The dark halls of that place had taken too long to escape from, and by the time Shrina was out she saw it was too late. Kengris was in the air, full dragon form, with Alicia flying at his side. Shrina cursed and ran to take flight.

A buzzing told her Richards was trying to get through. Maybe he had been for some time, but the comms hadn't worked below. She answered, quickly filling him in on the situation.

"Your team didn't like being left behind," he replied. "But... I'll send them coordinates."

"Be fast about it," she replied. "Please."

"You know I will. Oh, and Shrina?"

"Yes?"

"Don't go it alone anymore. This is a group effort."

"Roger that."

She was flapping with all her might, but Kengris and Alicia were gaining distance away from her. This wasn't working. Out of nowhere, missiles came, shooting at all three of them! Ahead, Kengris swooped and came up, blasting them with lightning before turning and taking down three jets as well. Alicia kept pushing on, clearly with a target in mind.

If Kengris was distracted, Shrina figured she might be able to get in there and try again with her sister. As soon as the thought went through her mind, though, a bolt of lightning shot back, only narrowly missing her.

Shrina growled, shooting in retaliation. Her shots went wide, the next bolt of lightning hitting her dead on. Only, instead of having its intended effect of killing her, it did something very strange—it caused the gun in her hands to explode, the blue energy within to expand around her and then, as she felt herself start to go limp... the blue moved into her and she was exploding through the air, then back together again on the dragon. It hadn't made sense. One second she was a ways back, the next she was collapsing onto his back, gripping onto his scales with her claws to keep from being thrown off as he dove and jerked about.

"Get off of him!" Alicia shouted, honing in on her sister, but Shrina willed herself onto the underside of the dragon and again the blue light took her.

Sure enough, she was on his underside, searching for openings in the armor as the dragon kept thrashing about in its attempt to get at her, she turned to see that Alicia was on him now, too, clawing her way over to his defense.

"I don't want to fight you!" Shrina shouted, scrambling out of the way of one of the dragon's massive claws that nearly got her. From this close, he was at a disadvantage, at least.

Alicia tore into Shrina's shoulder with her claws, attempting to pull her away from Kengris. In spite of the pain, Shrina held tight until the dragon had turned over, so that she was able to roll with her sister's attack and not lose her footing on the dragon. Then the two of them were up, standing as they went at each other with strikes. A front kick from Alicia was followed by her spinning her wings and nearly cutting into Shrina with the horns that she now had protruding from her arms, just like Shrina's did.

Gusts of wind threatened to throw them off, one pulling Shrina up into the air. She angled her wing to dive back down, managing to get a handhold on the dragon's scales near the base of his hind leg. Alicia let go in order to turn her attention toward slamming into her sister. The two grappled, the dragon unable to do anything about it at first.

Skimming the tops of the trees, the dragon was fast heading towards the ground, tearing through the branches that were now slapping at Shrina and Alicia as they fought. One took Shrina's leg out, and she fell into a kick to her head that sent her flying off towards the ground below. The dragon and Alicia took off into the sky again as Shrina recovered and launched herself back into the sky to follow them.

She had nearly caught up, when flashes of lightning erupted from the dragon's mouth again. He turned to fight her off, but she dug down between two hills, out of his sight. When she came back up the two were farther off in the distance, apparently more concerned with reaching their destination than fighting her.

There, my daughter, Kengris' voice shook through the mental connection as he veered down, plummeting into the ground.

Behind them and in the sky, an assault was incoming, likely led by Shrina's team. All she had to do was hold out and to ensure that nothing crazy happened to Alicia before they arrived. Alicia had landed next to Kengris, helping him up as he transformed into his gigantic humanoid form. The two took off in a mixture of running and flying, then descended down a decline and into a massive cave.

Shrina followed suit, confused as to what was going on. When she reached the top of the decline and looked down, she became even more confused. Kengris had become a dragon again, only to start slamming himself into the rocky side of the hill. Over and over, at times using his tail as a whip, others, going in with his entire body. Lightning bolts shot out from him to help in the job, but his body was doing more damage. Finally, a rumbling sounded like an earthquake. Rocks fell, giving way to what appeared to be a cave, partially hidden by trees.

They had come for something inside of that cave. A cave that very much reminded her of the one they had found along with the caverns near the Yellow River in Iran. Something the vampires were looking for.

Indeed, vampires emerged from nearby, some joining him, kneeling before their god returned, while others began shouting orders to take up defensive positions, pointing to the sky.

A glance back showed Shrina that her troops had arrived. It was time for war, but she needed to get into that cave and stop Kengris from whatever it was he was up to. The dragon shifted to his man form again, taking Alicia and disappearing from view.

The two sides clashed, vampires and military. Shrina made a beeline for the cave. Explosives went off nearby, setting vampire limbs rolling across the ground. Sounds tore through the trees, and screaming of the soldiers came as a group of vampires overtook them. Each side had ships by that point, along with weapons capable of taking them down. She had to wonder when the last time the soil had seen such courage might have been, dodging left to avoid an assault pod as it tore through the ground and exploded. She leapt up, thrust herself forward and through the smoke, then dive-bombed the engines. She landed in a roll, and was up sprinting to catch up with Kengris and her sister.

What she found within wasn't the numerous caverns she'd expected, but a simple ledge that led down to what appeared to be some old command room from a ship. Metal rose up on half of the walls, old torn apart command center screens littering the cave. But there, rising up out of the ground, the two sides of it looked like a metal gate. It reminded her of the images she had seen of what they had found on Mars, the gate that had opened the entryway to the stars, the one which Trent and the others had gone through.

Alicia and Kengris stood at the edge of each side of the gateway, one on the left and one on the right. Then they reached out a hand toward each other as blue light flashed from her fingertips meeting blue lightning from his. They formed a bond, a bond that activated the gateway. Before her eyes, Shrina watched the empty space form into liquid before clearing to show images.

First there was empty space. Then stars, followed by large red eyes. Blue energy around the edges shifted, and she realized Kengris was muttering something. Coordinates? Again the image shifted, this time showing a desert planet. Sand burst up as a huge sand worm emerged, leaping out of a hole and promptly diving into another, vanishing from view. Shrina pulled back in horror, imagining the sand worm coming up to get her in that cave. But the next image drew her forward, because she was looking at Trent. Oddly, he stood on a plateau with dragons flying around. Could this be something other than a gateway? She shook her head, trying to clear it and focus on what she was seeing, but by then the image was gone.

One more image showed, and then Shrina knew she would have her sister. It was a team, pushing through a sandstorm. They turned back, seemed to see through the portal, and one took his helmet off.

Marick.

It was the time to act, Shrina had no doubt. Throwing herself over the ledge, she swooped down on Alicia and tackled her away from the gate, then had her. Nowhere else to go, they charged back up and out as the dragon roared behind them, transforming to give chase. Outside, Shrina pulled her sister around to the side of the cave, where a hill gave way to climbing areas and crevices that she figured might be great for hiding in.

They slid over a half-broken portion of the path, coming to a stop at the bottom. From there, they could hear the sounds of the roaring dragon and the screaming of the people above. More fighting and explosions.

Every part of Shrina wanted to take her sister and run, to get her to safety. But there was a look in Alicia's eyes, a look that said she felt the same about the situation as Shrina, A feeling that was at odds with her survival instincts.

"We have to stop him," Alicia said. "That was… it was Marick. I have to go to Marick."

"I know." Eyes scouring the surrounding rocks and drop-offs, Shrina had little hope in regard to the safety of their current hiding spot. "I have friends here. We can fight."

"Then we fight."

Alicia and Shrina pushed off from the rocks, using their wings as they turned to catch the wind and fly back up to the top. When they arrived, the Dragon was beginning to engage with the military forces. The ships were scattered across the battlefield, U.S. forces trying to use them as cover. There was only one move here. One way to end this with as little bloodshed as possible. Without hesitation, Shrina motioned to her sister to stay back while she charged forward, circling in the air above the dragon, and then she let her wings catch her to glide down.

"Enough," Shrina said, shouting and pushing with the same mental strength that allowed her to free the minds of vampires—at least when Kengris wasn't nearby. "This is between the two of us."

All vampires paused, turning to look at her, causing some to fall. A moment later, the Marines were silent too, their assault stopping long enough to see what was happening.

Kengris eyed her, then transformed into his human form. "You...? You are nothing to me."

"Then show the others. Stomp me into the ground... finish me."

"Gladly."

He charged. She braced herself. Out of the corner of her eye she saw Trish at the ready, Irithu and the others circling up, preparing for her signal. It wasn't going to happen, though. Not while she had a chance.

And thanks to her new ability, she believed she could do this. Kengris was halfway to her when she focused on that blue light that had entered her, then concentrated on a spot where he was about to step. Waiting to the count of two, as his foot left the spot, she made it happen. Blue flight flashed and she was gone from where she had been standing, instead appearing behind him and grabbing the back of his wings as she kicked out at his legs and twisted.

The result was Kengris slamming into the ground, Shrina going with him to connect with an elbow and then two quick knees before using the power again to flash away and reappear ten paces away. Crouched and at the ready, she watched him roar in pain and anger, then come at her. As far as she knew, the power she had was similar to the exoskeleton with teleportation power that Cody had been wearing. Which meant that the power supply was limited.

She couldn't keep this up forever. Reaching deep within and trying to gauge how much of that energy was left, she figured she had at least one more in her. The only problem was, when she tried again and this time went for a spot in the air to come at him with a flying knee, when the knee connected he wasn't fazed. He caught her, knee still in his face, and brought her down head-first into his own knee. Quick, dull pain... taking over her limp body.

Dropping her to the ground, he lifted his hands and roared. Vampires cheered.

Every voice in her head screamed for her to quit, to give in to the pain. He wasn't attacking, though, but was playing up the moment, basking in his glory, their worship. All he cared about was his ego. Being above all. Perfect.

She pushed herself up, kneeling, but met Trish's eye,

then Alicia's, hoping they got the hint. Don't move. Don't attack.

"You see, petulant child," Kengris said, stepping back over to her and stopping to leer down at her kneeling form. "You should have let it be, taken the power I gave you... accepted my daughter's spirit into you. Now, what? You would try to steal her from me?" He gestured at Alicia, and as he did so the blue flared to life in her eyes again.

"No," Shrina replied, her voice barely a whisper. Then she was thrusting up, head right into his groin as hard as she could, then grabbing both legs and heaving so that he was on his back. She spun, still gripping one leg so that the ankle snapped, and then she remembered the gun, the one from the room.

Point blank. Three shots to the face. Flesh... gone.

His body stopped twitching a couple of seconds later, going limp. As it did, a new sort of pull called from him. Not one to worry about, but one that told her she was about to become one happy camper. Stepping toward his dying form, she reached out. Sure enough, the pull responded. It came in the form of his body convulsing first, then blue light streaming out of him like a torrential downpour, only sideways and funneling directly into her hand.

Finally, as the last of the blue light entered her, Kengris was gone. His body withered up until it was the size of a normal man. Everything around Shrina seemed to be happening in slow motion as she let the power surge through her. Much like the blue from before, she sensed abilities she couldn't begin to comprehend. Not yet.

At this moment, she needed to stop the fighting. With a wave of her hand, the red from the eyes of the vampires faded.

"They're on our side now," she said, voice quiet but resonating over the battlefield.

The soldiers still held their weapons at the ready, glancing around with uncertainty. Then Veles stepped out from a ship as it lowered to hover near Shrina. He was geared up and in one of the fancy exoskeletons; they all looked to him.

"Stand down," he called out. "It looks like we just won this battle."

Cheers and shouts of "Oorah!" echoed off of the surrounding rocks.

Pride rose through Shrina, but it was nothing compared to the joy of seeing Alicia running up to her, wrapping her arms around her neck.

"I'm so sorry!" Alicia said, pulling back, a hand to her mouth. "What... what did I do?"

"It wasn't you," Shrina replied. "He had some sort of power over you."

"We dig the new look," Irithu said, approaching with Trish. The others were greeting some of the other vampires—apparently a lot of them had known each other from before this whole fiasco with the dragon and Cody using the genetic modifications to control them.

"Pete!" Trish exclaimed, and ran over to a vampire

who was on the ground, one leg missing and half of his left arm hanging off.

"Her brother," Irithu explained to the others, then jogged over to help.

Shrina knew there was no healing from that, but there were other options. A cyborg vampire could come in handy, she imagined. They could take care of him for now.

"Oh, they... stayed on me," Alicia said, noticing the wings now, flapping them clumsily.

"You won't have to be jealous of me, at least," Shrina teased, flapping her own wings and earning a couple of shouts of surprise from nearby soldiers and Marines.

"Indeed." Alicia chuckled, eyeing Shrina with a look that showed she wasn't quite sure she was ready to be a demi-dragon, but wasn't about to complain with Shrina standing right there.

"Come on," Shrina said, putting an arm around her sister. "Let's meet the troops. I have questions for Veles, and we need to show him something."

30

TRENT, REMALD

As far as Trent was concerned, the main enemy was taken out. Both of them, actually, considering that the High Drin had been sent through a portal to some other part of space, while Ohklon was now their prisoner. It wasn't likely the Drin was dead, as Trent had seen dragons go into space and survive without protection, so the High Drin could in theory be out there, finding a place to land or getting help nearby. The portal didn't likely lead to just any old random place, after all.

Still, they were both out of the picture for now, at least.

Trent took the duty of escorting Ohklon back to the prison - one of the old dragon carcasses where he had first seen Ohklon, along with Feras. Feras carried them both on her back, and from his high perch there he watched the others move into the city down below, routing a group who had been putting up a fight against the royal family. It wasn't much of a fight, by that point, and the Ajargons cleaned up the streets nicely with their dragon fire, blasters, and even blades.

We did well, Feras noted. *You did well.*

"Thank you."

They watched as Merax and the prince rose up in dragon form, taking on the last of the enemy shifters. Two dragons tearing into a third was a sight to behold, and when the enemy hit the ground, dead, a roar went up that could be heard all the way out to where Feras was starting to touch down.

Between two hills, the eye socket of a dragon's skull showed. Not easily noticeable by the untrained eye, as it could have been a random cave. Trent, however, had come to both recognize the skull and to be able to sense the power emanating from it.

"When you die, will you be one of these?" he asked Feras as he and Ohklon slid off, the latter starting to come to, but groggy.

She eyed him, then transformed back to herself. "How morbid."

"I mean—"

"Just giving you a hard time. No, unless I live to become one of the Immortals." She grimaced, likely realizing he had no idea what she meant by that. "When one of our kind advances to the ultimate level of being able to master the light, they can, in theory, live forever. Until killed, that is."

"Which explains why there are none among us?"

She cocked her head. "The prince, actually, claims to have attained this level of enlightenment."

"We have many," Ohklon muttered, eyes unfocused, but determined. "And they will feast on your flesh when they arrive."

Trent scowled at him, but then turned back to Feras. "Is it true?"

"It's not unlikely," she admitted. "Not the feast on your flesh part—we won't let that happen."

"I should hope not." He forced a laugh, to which Ohklon shook his head.

"When the day comes—" Ohklon was cut off by a solid punch from Feras. Strong enough to send him back into an unconscious state that required Trent to bend at the knees to catch the man.

"Whoa." Trent looked at her, impressed.

"Sorry, just… wanted him to shut up." She motioned toward the eye, and they entered.

They continued in, moving along the dragon's spine as Trent had with the other one, and finally were at the heart. Black, but not as dry as the other. A dull, purple light emitted from it.

"Before we leave him, I'd like to try something." Trent knelt in front of Ohklon. Focusing on his breathing, he tried going into the man's mind, as the man had done to him. Sure enough, he was in. A barrage of images came at Trent. He was in a different time, with myriad dragons soaring overhead. Ohklon, kneeling, broken, being lifted back up by a man who exuded power. Bald. Gleaming, blue eyes. The man wore thick space armor of gold and gray, and looked into Ohklon's eyes, telling him he would be someone again, that he would rise up with the Apophian. Leaning in, he nearly pressed his lips to Ohklon's, but instead breathed into the man. The breath took hold, blue, and when Ohklon opened his eyes in this vision, his eyes were completely blue, too. The other turned and walked off, becoming a dragon as he went.

A moment later, Ohklon was transforming, too, then running and leaping, flying as a dragon among the others.

Back in the dragon carcass with Feras, Ohklon's gaze went hollow, eyes rolling back, and he started to spasm. Trent was vaguely aware of this, watching the man from inside his mind. The dragon was right there for the taking, and so Trent took a mental hold and yanked.

A flurry of black and green shot at him, the dragon transforming to more of the light, all of it flooding into Trent and then filling him from the inside and moving out. Before he knew what was happening, he was turning, wings spread—he was the dragon!

But he dismissed it almost as quickly, staring down at the ground to wonder if that had been a dream. Judging by the look Feras was giving him when his eyes met hers again, it had all actually happened.

He had become a dragon.

"I guess that means you're ready," Feras said, eyes wide. It had been as unexpected to them as it had been to him.

"We'll see," he replied, turning to leave Ohklon to his new prison.

31

ESPINOZA, KRASTIAN

On the other side of the gate, Espinoza and the others came out into yet another storm. There was a bit of a drop on the other side, only a few feet, but onto rock. The landing wasn't bad for those in armor, but Marick cursed. He was tough, but with the burns already making him hurt, his reaction was understandable.

"Watch out for sandworms!" Ellins shouted, starting to guide them all to some nearby rocks.

"Any idea how that portal closes?" Kim asked.

"Not from our side," Espinoza replied, wishing he had thought about that before coming through. Maybe they could have pulled out all the energy stones but one, or tried something else to shut it off as they went through. Not that it would have mattered much, because the Reshodan could open it again whenever they wanted.

As the wind roared around them, they pushed

towards the hills. Halfway there, though, Marick turned and grabbed Espinoza's arm.

"Where's Ruan?"

"She... didn't make it." Espinoza pulled his arm free. "And before you say it, no. There was no healing from that."

Marick blinked, processing that information, then nodded. The curses he muttered as he marched on carried back faintly in the wind. No sandworms came, and every time Espinoza glanced back, he was relieved to see no Goldies. It wasn't until they reached the base of the hill that the portal vanished, but by then the group had found a spot where rocks rose up on either side, a bit of a cavern within. A spot where they could form a new base, at least until they figured out where they were.

Climbing up and back into the cavern, they finally stopped, staring out at the storm as it faded.

"They didn't come through," Kim noted.

"And the sandworms didn't attack." Espinoza figured it was as good of a time as any to tell them his theory. "The Goldies... I think they're formed from the Reshodan soldiers. Like, they shed their skin or something and are able to use the gold energy to control it, send it as proxies of themselves into battle."

"That's insane." Marick frowned, refusing to accept that.

"And amazing," Kim admitted.

A beep sounded, and she turned, fidgeting with something. Meanwhile the rest of the group stared out at those rocks, all likely feeling the same sense of loss and hopelessness as Espinoza.

"What now?" Franco asked. He stood up and strode over to the edge, it seemed to take a piss. As he started, he called over his shoulder, "What's next?"

"Next...?" Marick looked around at each of them. "We're stranded, surrounded by hostiles. I don't know what to say."

"Earth will come," Kim said. She held up her fore-arm, swiping to make a screen appear larger, hovering there for the group to see. "I set this up before we went —like a smart watch, it notifies me if we get communi-cations. Meaning, at least our comms equipment is still working, and can't be too far from us."

"Are they saying...?" Espinoza asked, staring at the message between the strange letters. He knew crypto, but the message seemed garbled.

"It might have gone through some changes, but..." Kim made some adjustments, then laughed. "Yes!"

As she laughed again, the screen changed, removing the extra letters and numbers. Hovering before them was a message as clear as it could be—Earth was sending reinforcements. They were coming to rescue the group.

"Espinoza, Kim, on me," Ellins said, gesturing them back. "We'll investigate the cavern, make sure we're safe while Marick and Franco keep watch. Then we'll set up base."

Espinoza wasn't about to argue with that, and didn't bother to hide his smile as Franco watched them go with a frown. Maybe he would start suspecting something was up with Espinoza and the two ladies, soon, but that would be a conversation for another time.

"So, we're doing this again?" Espinoza asked as they advanced farther into the cavern, once they had left the others far behind and used their mounted lights to check the shadowed corners and back walls.

"Excuse me?" Ellins said, scanning the area. "I don't know what you're talking about."

Except, as she leaned her rifle against the wall, she turned and started to remove her armor.

"Yeah, me neither." Kim winked, catching on, but working to remove Espinoza's armor first. They could be attacked at any moment, pursued by the Goldies most likely.

But that didn't deter them. It just meant they couldn't waste time.

Work hard, play hard—the way of champions, Espinoza thought as Kim leaned in to kiss him, armor finally off, and then Ellins came up behind, lips on his neck, hands roaming along his chest, down to his abs, and continuing down.

32

SHRINA, VIRGINIA

"You had something to show me?" Veles asked, following Shrina and Alicia through the tunnels and caverns toward that old, torn up command room. Two of his men followed, both equally decked out.

"Yes, but first..." Alicia turned, eyeing the others, weighing them. "What was your connection to Set?"

"Excuse me?"

"First your nephew ends up being behind all of this, then I find out you and Set were connected in the New Origins days." She stepped closer, not afraid to show she meant business. "I want the truth, right here and now."

"You're being absurd."

"Before I show you this," she gestured down the tunnels, to the area that led to the portal. "You need to come clean. What was your involvement?"

He glared at her, but to his credit held up a hand to stop one of his men when the guy's hand went for his gun.

"Set was my right hand, once upon a time," Veles admitted. "But he disappeared. We knew that we had a mole on the inside. What we didn't know was that they were in any way using our experiments to control the vampires, or that the dragon was in any sense awake. I certainly didn't know Cody was involved, or would have been the first to take him out."

"You swear to this?" Shrina glanced at her sister, who was looking puzzled.

"I do," Veles replied.

"One thing, though," Alicia cut in. "I don't follow how Cody did it."

"My guess," Shrina replied, "is that Kengris formed a connection as he did with you and me. Worked through Cody as a proxy, talking to him through his mental connection, and was therefore likely to reach out to the super soldiers throughout the world. Those who had been injected with the super-soldier serum that had been made thanks to his DNA."

Veles nodded. "It would check out."

"Sounds like a damn fairy tale," one of his men said, shaking his head.

"You go through a gateway to the stars, and think life will go on as we knew it?" Veles chuckled, shaking his head. "We're pilgrims, my man. This is the first step toward a new universe as we know it."

"And on that note…" Alicia nodded.

Shrina took a breath, then motioned for Veles and his men to follow her.

"What is it?" Veles asked, eyeing it with wonder.

"Far as I know," Shrina shrugged, "the Mayflower."

That piqued his curiosity. Stepping in after her, the gasp that he let out filled the otherwise silent room. Even without the two there to fuel it, the portal was active, shimmering, now on an empty point in space.

Watching him approach the portal was like watching a child approach Santa for the first time. Timid, maybe a bit afraid, but ultimately infatuated and in love.

"At last," Veles said, voice full of awe.

"Excuse me?" Alicia asked.

"You knew about this?" Shrina shared a nervous look with her sister. "And what exactly is… this?"

"A portal to other worlds, other galaxies…" Veles shook his head, amazed. He motioned to his men as a commotion sounded outside, more following and carrying cases.

"We have to close it," Shrina said.

"No." Veles held his arms out, exoskeleton extending, forming armor that wrapped out to cover his limbs.

Others entered, and seemed to have been briefed on what they would find. Some had the helmets assigned to Marines with the Space Fleet, one handing a helmet to Veles. They had rifles larger than the DD4s, a type that Shrina had never seen. Other weapons as well, including what looked like bombs, exoskeletons with that blue energy that Set had used to teleport, and more.

"Answers will follow in time, my dear," Veles said, hitting her with a shot that sent her into spasms on the floor, then wouldn't let her stand. "But for now, simply know that your time will come."

"What are you doing?" Alicia demanded.

"It's too dangerous out there to let Earth's fate rest on the abilities of our Marines. That's where me and mine step in. We mean to conquer these others, to show them who is in charge. When it's time, we will unite the worlds and emerge as Earth's champions… and then some."

The look of greed in his eyes sent a chill up Shrina's spine, and in that moment, his eyes flashed gold. As he and his followers entered the portal, Shrina couldn't help but be glad to be done with them. He was going into the unknown and, as far as she knew, would end up dead before long.

Good riddance.

As soon as the last of them was through, the portal shifted, the series of rune-like characters changing along with it. Coordinates, Shrina noted, and glanced back at her sister. Finally able to move, Shrina picked herself up and threw her arms around Alicia. For now, all that mattered was that they were together again.

This portal could be the key to helping Trent, maybe reaching him or Marick, she wasn't sure. There was much to figure out, and the government had the original portal, or gateway as they called it.

When the time came, Shrina and Alicia would make the right choice, she had no doubt. Together, they walked out to find the rest of their team, to prepare for what would come next.

33

TRENT, REMALD

N ow that the city of Realt was at peace, Trent had finally had the chance to get some real sleep. Dreams came of flying as a dragon, of swooping around as Feras joined him, the two of them wrapped together as one, and then transforming to light that shot out across the planet. He awoke to find Feras at his side, staring into his eyes.

"Did you seriously just watch me as I slept?" he asked, stretching as he sat up.

"I have news," Feras said, taking his hand and guiding him to the window, where they could see the silver prince flying as he so loved to do.

"Let me guess," Trent cocked his head at her, trying to clear his fuddled mind of the grogginess of sleep, "you're secretly his sister? Princess of all these people?"

She frowned, then laughed. "Excuse me?"

"No?"

"Not remotely. Not only no, but definitely not. Me, related to them?" She shook her head vehemently.

"What then?"

"They've appointed Merax and the Ajargons royal guardians of Remald. Merax has invited you to join their ranks, and I told him you would accept."

Trent stood tall, finding his chest puffing out at the honor. Of course he would accept, but... "What does that mean for the two of us?"

"That's the real news. Or... question?" Her eyes stared up at his, wavering. "We've only known each other a short time, and I don't know how it works on Earth, but here... when you know, you know."

"Holy shi..." He chuckled, shaking his head. "What are you saying?"

"I know with everything in me, so believe it's right. Trent, I want you to be with me."

"As in... I mean, are you asking me to marry you?" He swallowed, finding his throat very dry. "To be your spouse? To share a life together, forever?"

She reached out, took his hand, and shook her head. "No, it's way too soon for that. But, I'm expressing how I feel. And inviting you to my bed."

"Oh." He swallowed again, then smiled as he repeated, "Oh!"

"The look on your face." She licked her lips, suddenly looking self conscious. "So...?"

"I accept." He took her hand to his mouth, pressing his lips to the back of it. "And by the way, I feel the same about you."

Feras waved a hand along his chest so that his robes faded to light that drifted to the floor and reformed as robes. As simple as that, he was nude, and just as simply, so was she. They took each other, kissing and making love, and when it was done both lay in each other's arms, simply enjoying the moment.

"This is where I belong," Trent said.

"Remald is a better place with you on it."

"I meant right here, holding you close."

She chuckled, leaned over to kiss him, and lay on top of him, eyes on his. "Together, we can do anything."

"Right now, or…?"

She hit him, playfully. "I don't mean in that way. But…" Her playful smile was interrupted by a knock on the door. "Yes?"

The door opened and a guard half-entered before realizing what he was walking in on. "My apologies."

"What is it?" She sat up, sheets to her chest.

"A meeting has been called," the guard said, averting his gaze. "In the throne room."

Feras shared a look of curiosity with Trent. As the guard departed, they started to get dressed. She seemed concerned, voicing more than once that the royal family rarely held such meetings, and soon they were on their way. As they had a room in the castle, it wasn't long before they reached the ornate, silver doors, opened by guards.

They entered the throne room and Yoldrok was the first to greet them, with Councilor Bligort there at his side. The two men apologized for all of the hassle they had caused, and welcomed Trent to the palace. He graciously accepted, letting bygones be bygones. Others were already gathered, with the queen and prince on their thrones. But first, Trent noticed Ezail, watching them.

"You're okay with this?" he asked her, stepping up to her side with Feras's arm in his.

Ezail smiled at her mom first, then at him. "It's an honor."

"Thank you," he replied, gave her a hug, and then turned back to see Merax and his top Ajargons moving up to the left of the thrones.

This clearly wasn't simply some award ceremony or after-action report, Trent noted. Everyone looked much too stern for either. When Gray and his followers entered, they were greeted with nods of acceptance, and then the doors were closed behind them.

The queen held up a hand, eyes roaming over the room. "Our people have fought bravely. Everyone here today has earned a spot in the inner circle..." She put her hand to her chest, glanced over her shoulder, and seemed unable to go on.

"We... have something to show you." The prince stood, ignoring the looks of annoyance from the queen, and gestured to guards behind him.

They moved quickly, going for the rear walls. Moving the walls sideways, one at a time, it became clear that the entire back wall of the throne room was like a divider, hiding what Trent now saw was some glowing force. When the last of the walls was removed, the sight was clear, and more confusing than Trent could've expected. Right there in the throne room was a portal. Similar to the gateway to the stars Trent and others had flown through to reach this other galaxy, though this one was smaller—but still larger than the one the High Drin had gone through. It took up the area from one wall to the other, rising up to be about two stories tall. It could easily fit a space ship through, and had an array of weapons aimed at it. Most confusingly, an image appeared within—one that was distorted like a rippling reflection in a pond, but shifted between images. At one moment it showed land like an empty desert, then open space, a couple of ships flying past. Large ships of alien designs like that of this planet but more fierce, and then the red eyes. As it shifted again, a strange, golden figure floated past, storm clouds taking up the image beyond.

"The portals are open," the prince said.

"Or just this one?" Feras asked.

He shook his head. "Others, too. We've sent scouts to check, and already the first have reported that it's true."

"Meaning?" Trent asked.

The prince eyed him as if he were a simple child, then stepped forward, hand out to indicate the portal.

"Once, there was a system of these interconnected portals which our people would use to traverse galaxies. We set up planets, inhabited them, and moved on to conquer others that were in need of guidance.

Some split off, eventually, after a protracted campaign to put an end to the conquering of others."

"He's familiar with that part of the story," Merax cut in.

Trent nodded, but still felt lost. "This is one of those portals?"

"Dormant many years," the prince said. "It is, and has only now been activated. After many years, the system is open—and that means we are in serious trouble."

AUTHOR NOTES

With book three finished, I hope you're ready and waiting for book four! I'll be working on it with all my heart and soul. In the meantime, can I ask a favor? Please review the books and spread by word of mouth! It all helps.

Also, be ready for audio. It's always fun to listen to a book after reading it, because the narrators bring their own magic to the experience.

Are you having fun here? Our team learned more about the dragon with Shrina, saw a hint at where Goldies come from along with the fact that peace won't come easy for Espinoza, but also had a blast kicking ass with Trent. Book four will bring us face to face with the exiles, explore more of the Goldies and delve into the fight with the Reshodan and their people.

All that is to say—stay tuned! I love writing, and hope you love what I'm putting out there.

Thank you for reading.

Justin

JOIN THE NEWSLETTER

And join the FB group!
https://www.facebook.com/groups/JustinSloan/

Printed in Great Britain
by Amazon

38227130R00175